I0546980

Trigger Warning:
Speaking Ill

COMPILED BY JOHN BALTISBERGER

EDITED BY CHRISTINE MORGAN
AND LISA TONE

TABLE OF CONTENTS

INTRODUCTION

CHANDLER MORRISON

"*I WANT YOU* to fuck me like I'm one of your dead girls."

It was when a woman said this to me in bed that the effects of *Dead Inside* on my life really became apparent to me. I remember thinking, *My God, what have I done?* Since its publication, it seems my name has become synonymous with necrophilia. Fans send me lewd memes about corpse-fucking over social media. I get tagged whenever a news article about a necrophile starts circulating (there's a fake one about a woman getting impregnated by a dead guy that seems to crop back up every few months). I've lost track of the number of times I've had to earnestly say to someone, "Well, no, actually, I don't have sex with dead girls."

This is my legacy.

Thus, when John approached me about writing the introduction to an anthology with a "disrespect the dead" theme, it wasn't as if I could decline. I'd been expecting a book of short stories largely centered around copulation with corpses, so I was pleasantly surprised to find the content of the manuscript to be varied and creative. The talent contained in the pages which follow—names both new and established—have come up with a vastly assorted smorgasbord of ways in which to disrespect the dead. Some corpses do indeed get an old-fashioned fucking, yes, but that doesn't even begin to scratch the surface of the depravity on display. My brow was constantly lifting as I perused the atrocities laid out in this book, and my brow does not often lift.

All of this led me to thinking . . . what is it about disrespecting the dead that stirs such visceral reactions in people? Myself, I've always thought our society places, perhaps, an undue and unhealthy amount of reverence on our dearly departed. In my 2017 novel *Hate to Feel*, the protagonist muses, "Death canonizes even the most awful of us. No one will speak ill of you when the dirt is still fresh upon your grave. It's only once the grass starts to grow that everyone remembers what a piece of shit you were."

The question remains . . . why? Why are the dead afforded so much more respect than the living? Americans will flock to a movie theater to watch Joe Action Hero mindlessly slaughter an endless legion of living, breathing humans, all while they cram their grinning maws with butter-slathered popcorn, but God forbid the corpses of any of those hapless grunts get defiled after the fact.

There's an assumed sanctity in death. "Don't speak ill of the dead," we say. But the living? Nah, they're fair game. We have such rituals around our dead. Such veneration. Such tradition. Anything which breaks that tradition, that spits in the face of those venerable rituals . . . this is seen as capital-B Bad.

Me? I don't know, I don't put that much stock in all of it. I don't care what happens to my corpse when I die. Bury me, cremate me, blow me up. Toss me in a ditch. Fuck me. What do I care? I'll be dead.

Maybe that's why I was able to enjoy the stories in this anthology. I just don't have as many hang-ups. If you're like me, there's certainly plenty here for you to appreciate.

And if not? If you're one of those who has a higher regard for the lifeless than the living?

Well.

Consider this your trigger warning.

STAY WITH ME:
A LOVE STORY

P.J. BLAKEY-NOVIS

I UNLOADED MYSELF across her breasts with a groan and a shudder, collapsing onto the bed beside Jennifer. She remained still, eyes closed, silent as ever. For a few minutes, I rested my head on her shoulder, ignoring the odours which escaped from her, and laid an arm across her stomach. I felt a wetness as some of the semen touched my skin, and I thought about my next task. In life, Jennifer had no objection to finishing our lovemaking sessions in this way. In death, she objects even less. I used to have the decency to wipe her down, and now I have to. The combination of my own fluids and the baby oil mixed with the makeup I spent so long applying causes it to run, revealing the greyish hue of old skin beneath.

Sliding open the bottom drawer on my bedside cabinet, I retrieved the necessary items once again– wet wipes, hand towel, concealer. I cleaned Jennifer carefully, wiping away the remains of my lust, before drying those areas. The most painstaking task is repairing the makeup, making Jennifer look as much like her former self as possible. It isn't only for my benefit, of course. Jennifer made a lot of effort with her appearance—she'd hate for me to let her look anything other than perfect.

The whole situation has been time-consuming, hard work, expensive, and, in all honesty, a huge learning curve. But that's marriage, right? A while ago, while things were still normal between us, we'd heard some Internet hoax about a law in Egypt permitting men to have 'farewell sex' with their dead wives, so long as it was within six hours of death. We'd joked about it, and Jennifer asked me if I would, telling me she wouldn't mind, what with her being dead and all.

"Depends how you died," I replied, deliberately not ruling the necrophilic act out completely. "I mean, if it was a car crash, I couldn't very well drag you from the wreckage and hop on at the side of the road." We laughed about that, inventing a number of scenarios. Perhaps oddly, the whole conversation got us quite worked up, and I recall the sex on that evening being particularly intense.

Jennifer didn't die in a car crash. Or any other kind of accident. She passed away peacefully in her sleep at the age of thirty-one. I'm sure there was a medical reason, of course, maybe a heart attack or massive stroke, but she has never been seen by anyone to investigate this. That morning was a blur, from the shock, to the fear I would somehow be blamed, to wondering what to do next. I suppose a therapist would say I was unable to let her go, and that seems to be true. Yes, things are different. Not better, not really worse, just different.

I found myself on autopilot for the rest of that day, researching preservation techniques, planning the required level of deception. Part of me knew that this wouldn't be a forever situation, and I pushed that worry to the back of my mind. Jennifer was doing temp work through an agency so wouldn't be missed there; it was quite common for people to drift in and out of that sort of work. There was only a sister to consider, Neve, but they only spoke every few weeks, and this was always via messages, something I could easily replicate. A time would come, I supposed, when I'd have to dispose of the body and claim she was missing, but that time wasn't now. Now, I had work to do.

Embalming techniques were easy enough to find online, and I soon had a handwritten list of bullet points: disinfect the skin, massage limbs to reduce stiffness from rigor mortis, fix the mouth into the desired position (for this, I rested one of Jennifer's larger dildos in her mouth in the hope the jaw would set in the ideal way). Formaldehyde would have been the best, of course, but I didn't hold the required permits to purchase such an item. I decided to settle for ethanol, almost as effective, available to anyone, and with free next-day delivery.

That first day was spent massaging Jennifer's corpse and using household disinfectant to clean every part of her, all the while doing my best to ignore my erection. She wasn't ready yet, and the wait only made me want her more. Much more.

An evening of reading scientific articles and watching YouTube videos had me mentally prepared for 'the main event.' It was going to be messy, smelly, and rather unpleasant. I reminded myself how it would all be worth it in the end, how Jennifer would be happy with her transformation if she knew. She'd told me she wanted to be with me forever–I was just giving her what she wanted. That night, I slept well, my clammy hand resting on Jennifer's cold stomach.

The following morning a large box arrived— apparently, no one had found anything strange about my order of ethanol, syringes, gauze, and other medical supplies. Positioning my lover in the bathtub, I set to work draining her blood. Downward slices on each arm, horizontal cuts across femoral arteries, and the tub began to turn red, albeit slowly. There was no beating heart to push the blood forth, and I squeezed and pushed at her body, trying to expel as much as possible. This wasn't as easy as I'd expected.

I took one of the largest syringes and began pumping her full of the ethanol, which, in turn, pushed the blood from her body. I was relieved I hadn't waited any longer as the blood was already thickening and would soon become too difficult to move. It took hours, but eventually, her arterial system was filled with the alcohol. I was on to the part which I dreaded . . release of gases and other liquids.

Taking the scalpel, I made an incision in Jennifer's abdomen, releasing some of the ethanol I'd worked so hard to inject. I felt around inside her, locating each organ in turn, puncturing them, and clearing out anything I found inside. As my hands reached inside her, my desire grew, but this was soon counteracted by the smell of bile and shit that I released from her. Cleaned, topped up with ethanol, and stitched back together, Jennifer was complete. I showered her down, dried her, disinfected once more, and moved her back to our bed (dildo still in her mouth).

The day had taken it out of me, and once I was satisfied everything was clean and looking (and smelling) as normal as possible, I stuck on a movie and fell asleep on the sofa.

Jennifer and I spent the next day together as I applied makeup. I painted her nails, brushed her hair, added eyeliner, and even popped out to purchase a few can of spray-on tan. The skin didn't look too bad yet, but I knew the colour would start to change within days and Jennifer wouldn't like to look that way. I had to keep her perfect, just as she had been in life.

The dildo idea had worked, and I applied what Jennifer had referred to as 'slutty red' lipstick to her mouth before entering it. The dryness was off-putting but easily fixed, selecting her favourite watermelon flavoured lube. It was quickly over, and I wondered about cleaning her mouth out, but there wasn't much I could do aside from a quick wipe with some wet wipes. I made a note not to get carried away with the mouth or she'd soon be too full to use.

Days turned into weeks, with me only leaving the

house for necessary items. Jennifer and I would spend days in bed; I'd read to her, we'd watch movies, I'd do her makeup every morning. I'm sure she was happy, and she must have known that I was. This is how things had to be, together and without the interference of other people. I'll admit that I used her body a bit too much, certainly more than she would have agreed to. Despite my massaging, Jennifer wasn't all that flexible, so my choice of position was quite limited.

After four weeks, everything changed. Jennifer had an odour I couldn't ignore, and we were coming into summer, so it would only get worse. My over-enthusiastic lovemaking had left every orifice full to the point of unusable. By the six-week point, I was reduced to spraying her with my seed from a distance before returning to sleep on the sofa. I felt as though I'd let her down and that our relationship may well be coming to an end.

I'd managed to keep up a reduced version of Jennifer's online life for a few weeks, but I'd neglected it recently. I didn't really think anyone would notice, but I was wrong, and this mistake would prove fatal, just not for me.

I suppose it was fortunate that I'd been expecting a delivery or I wouldn't have answered the door. Although fortunate may not be the right word. I doubt our unannounced visitor feels very lucky now. As much as the smell from Jennifer was unpleasant, I had become accustomed to it to a point. I certainly didn't expect it to be so noticeable from the front door.

"Neve?" I said, the sunlight behind her causing me to squint as it tried to cut through some of the grim darkness I'd found myself living in.

"Where's my sister?" she asked, taking a step forward. "And what the fuck is that smell? It smells like someone died in here!"

"Plumbing," I managed weakly. It was the first thing that came to mind. Neve took another step, now inches from my face.

"I want to see Jennifer," she stated, her eyes darting into the bleakness beyond.

I had to make a decision, and the options quickly came to me—deny her entry and wait for the police to visit, or let her in. I chose the latter. After all, she wanted to see her sister, it was what she had asked for.

"She's not well," I said. "She's in bed." I must have looked upset as Neve appeared to soften, concern etching her face.

"What's wrong with her?" she asked.

"I don't know. Go up and see her, if you like."

Neve passed me and made her way up the stairs, covering her mouth and nose as she went. Silently, I locked the front door and slipped the key into my pocket. I was halfway up the stairs when I heard Neve's scream. I entered the bedroom to find her standing over Jessica, eyes wide, a phone in her shaking hands.

"What have you done?" she gasped, taking a step back as I approached.

"Oh my god, Neve! I didn't kill her! How could you think that?"

7

"I . . . need to go," she replied, unmoving, waiting for my permission.

I didn't kill Jennifer, I never would do such a thing. I just ensured we would have more time together, like she always said she wanted. Neve wanted to see Jennifer, so I let her, but now I needed to take action. Jennifer used to mourn the fact that she wasn't closer to her sister, but now they could spend all the time they wanted together. I was making sure she got what she desired.

When it came to Neve, I took a different approach. Draining Jennifer's blood had been challenging—a beating heart would help immensely. There was a scuffle, a few blows to Neve's head, and I had her in the bathtub. I made the same incisions, bleeding her out like fucking cattle. My erection made itself clear, and I didn't stop myself—Jennifer would want me to be happy. I rinsed away the mix of blood and semen and set to work with the preservation technique. Perhaps it would go better this time, maybe all I needed was practice. Jennifer always wanted more friends, and now I could make her as many as she'd like.

Redemptrix

Jay Wilburn

MARY, THE MOTHER of Jesus and a bunch of other dudes, was a slut, a whore, and a total cock tease, if you believed what people around Scully, Alabama said. Her nickname was Virgin Mary ever since the story got around that she tricked her daddy into believing she got pregnant the first time without having sex, like a tiger slug or some miracle. Some said it was her daddy who got her pregnant, so he was fine with that bullshit story given the alternatives. Others said it was God or an angel that knocked her up. Maybe aliens did it, like the dudes that waited around the Home Depot parking lot for day work. Didn't help that she gave the boy a Latino name.

Mary had been steady with a dude for most of the rest of the kids. He worked in construction and even had the mystery boy with the Spanish name helping out around the sites. Stepdaddy wasn't in the picture anymore that Easter after Jesus got lynched up on the hill the kids called Fuckhead. No telling why it happened beyond the evil of original sin, and only

9

Mary knew the truth about most of this stuff, which she pondered in her heart and kept to herself.

Fuckhead was mostly made of red clay and eroded away to ragged cliffs on three sides. From the top of it, you could see into Georgia and Tennessee where Scully butted up to the corner of the state. At night, kids drank up there, looking out on the lights in different states, believing the Devil as he whispered tempting things about being able to get out of that dead end town one day.

All this could be yours, kiddo.

What they did to her boy up there wasn't abundantly clear, but the possibilities had been gossiped about in the best Scully tradition. At the end of it, he was dead and ruined. That played over and over in her head as she slept in that Easter morning until the angel grabbed her by the throat to wake her ass up.

Her eyes flew open, and her vision blurred either from lingering sleep or impeded blood flow. She saw more eyes than a single face should hold, all leering down at her over her bed. Shapes that made no sense for a body. No halo around the fucked up head of the thing straddling her in the sheets twisted around her. So big, the beast had to hunch over to fit inside the trailer with its wings all bent around the curve of the ceiling behind it. Wings that looked more fleshy than feathery.

"Don't be afraid, bitch." It growled at her loud enough to shake the trailer on its blocks. Anyone outside who hadn't gone to morning service would come up with a good story as to why Virgin Mary's trailer was rocking before her son was even properly in the ground.

"What do you want now, you plucked chicken?" Her tongue swelled in her mouth, and she took care not to bite it. "I haven't seen you much since I kicked meth."

"You might as well have stuck with it. You were more interesting back then."

Angels smelled a little like cum but cleaner. Maybe a little like pool chemicals. Or like they were backed up with nowhere to deposit their spunk. She had the impression some of them wanted to fuck her, if they could get away with it.

"Where the hell were you when they killed my boy?"

"Watching. Where were you?"

"I've never gone anywhere."

He let go of her and climbed off. He backed up two thundering steps and crouched in the kitchen area. His gnarled wings swept magnets and old kiddy artwork off her fridge on one side and scattered potlids off shallow counters on the other. Wasn't the first time some asshole scattered her shit after getting off her.

She sat up, feeling her pulse in her eyes and waiting for a dark dizziness to recede.

"We're sending you somewhere now."

"Another poke from God? He's not as satisfying as people think." She untangled herself from sheets that smelled of dirty cum and stood up before she was ready. Mary managed not to fall, and some mornings, that was a great victory. This was one of those mornings, by God and Sonny J.

"He isn't done either. You'll be transformed, Mary. A new creation. A new creature."

She rolled her eyes and stood without bothering to cover herself. The angel stared with dull disinterest. Maybe this backed up messenger didn't want to fuck her after all. If he knew how much effort it took to keep her balance, he might have been more impressed.

"A new exhibit for Sky Daddy's mutant menagerie?"

"Whatever you want to call it." The angel shrugged, denting the trailer in three places and popping one of the small windows out of its frame. The yammer of a barking dog came through more clearly. The angel continued, "Time to be born again. Time to pass through the womb and birth canal a second time. Time for the Redeemer to rise."

"My son was the Redeemer, or that was the bill of goods you sold me when I still was a virgin. Now he's dead."

"We'll see." The angel winked. "You'll be the Redemptrix."

She narrowed her eyes. "Do I charge by the hour?"

"It's the feminine form of redeemer."

She shook her head. "That's not what it sounds like."

The angel waved a finger. "See for your own self."

Mary cramped up tight and there was blood. It flowed from more than one hole.

A violent wind swirled through the trailer. Wadded tissues spotted with blood, crumbs of hardened food hidden around the edges of the living space, dead roaches not so hidden, and chips of lead scraped and pricked like particles in a sandstorm.

The sheets she tried to grab up to hold over herself

shredded away in her fingers and joined the debris of the storm. The door popped its latch and then slipped a hinge to bang against the weathered wood of the railing outside. That relieved some of the building pressure inside, but not enough. The metal shell of the place crinkled, bulged, and stressed white at the seams.

Her body shifted and contorted in lycanthropic transformation. Instead of growing more hair, she shed it off everywhere except the silky mane of her head. Better than waxing. Her joints and bones cracked and hummed as she grew taller. Blood seeped from every fold of skin. Stretch marks raised purple but then smoothed out again to unnaturally bright porcelain shades across her skin.

Metal screamed from all sides of her as fissures opened in the sides and top of her home at the weak points. Her place was nothing but weak points. Once it started coming apart, the roof unzipped all around and every surface folded away from every other. Her possessions flew to every minor degree between the compass points.

Just as she thought her body would come apart next, leather straps studded with dull spikes wrapped around her nakedness. The leather supports covered nothing but lifted and accentuated every curved and weighty bit of her that might spark desire in all men and most women. It was just in time too because fat deposits swelled her breasts, ass, and upper thighs.

As Mary squinted against the dissipating debris of the divine dust devil around her, she felt her enhanced parts to ascertain herself of their reality. Everything was plump and perky, natural and perfect in equal measure, despite those traits being opposites. Her breasts were magnificent, but who wants to waste time describing breasts when they aren't the main thrust of the story?

A leather shaft formed in her right fist. It was thick, black, and veiny, so she was sure it was something else until the leather braided itself off the end and snaked to the floor in a long whip between her new boots, the only real clothing she wore.

As the wind died away, leaving her and the angel standing on a barren platform, the long hair on her head tied off in a high pony as stout as her new stature.

"And what am I supposed to do with all this?" she asked in a still small voice.

"Save the world," the angel said with the roll of all his eyes. "Make fucking miracles as women are always required to do."

Fucking miracles.

A couple local bitches stuck their heads out to see if the storm had passed. They lingered to check up on other folks' business.

"Maybe I don't think the world is worth saving anymore. Maybe God and His angels should do more of the heavy lifting."

"Mary, it never ceases to amaze me how often people pray for shit, but the moment an angel shows up to drop it in their lap, they don't believe it or want it. That's why God keeps using signs and hints so often. All these tea leaf and Holy Spirit games people want to play."

She looked down at herself as much as she could around her ridiculous tits. She could already see her tattoos were missing. That ink wasn't cheap. Eyes back on the angel, she said, "I don't remember asking for this anymore than the first time God fucked me."

"You asked for something to be done about your dead son, didn't you? Well, you're the Redemptrix now, dear. You fucked a savior into to life once. Time to fuck with death."

She narrowed her eyes. "Speak plain, asshole. It's cold out here, and I'm wearing ribbons."

"Go to him. Raise the dead. You'll know how when you get there. The world needs saving whether it deserves it or not."

The angel ascended like a rocket, knocking the blocks out from under the floor and bringing her the rest of the way down to the hardpacked earth.

The birds tittered at one another in beautiful anger. Under that, she heard the whispers from other doorways and nailed-together porches—the still small voices of gossips. And their eyes. The judging eyes of women and the leering eyes of men fell upon a body and a life she hadn't asked for.

"Nothing good ever came out of Scully, Alabama," Mary muttered.

Her fist tightened around the veiny grip of her whip, and she put it to use. Her first act as the Redemptrix was vengeance. She slashed back and forth as she marched through the trailer park. The rough braid of leather sheared across eyes, leaving them in their sockets but ruining their surfaces in scarred blindness. If they tried to blink closed, she tore away the thin membranes of their lids. If they covered their faces with their hands, then she lashed them hard enough to break off the fingers, sever the hands, and clean away the front of their skulls with the force of the attack. Tearless weeping, gnashing of teeth, and empty threats of lawsuits filled the morning air in her wake, driving out the songs and threats of the birds.

One last man fell to his knees and held up his hands to her at the edge of the road. He begged for mercy, offered to lick her boots, offered to eat her ass, if she just let him keep his eyes. He said all this as his cock swelled erect in the front of his shorts.

Mary snapped the whip, tearing away his member in an ejaculation of dark blood. It wasn't that impressive once exposed, even before it shriveled, spinning away in the air. She lashed out again, ripping his head from his shoulders. The body slumped to one side on the shoulder of the road. The head stopped its roll short of the center line and licked over the chapped upper lip before it stilled. The eyes she let him keep turned glassy.

A moment later, an F150 squashed the head like a pumpkin. The driver let off the gas as he and his passenger admired her in their mirrors. Wisdom prevailed, and he laid down on the accelerator again, saving his own life that Easter as he left Scully behind.

She marched down the center of the street between the empty shops downtown.

Early services let out at just the wrong time. Men and women in light shades and pastel colors stopped to point and whisper. Messages of forgiveness and grace were forgotten in an instant. Women covered the eyes of children once they got their senses back. Mary could smell the lust off of them. Then, they started to whisper, and it hurt her head.

She thought about letting out the ponytail to help her aching head but then turned to her whip again instead. She left their eyes but opened their bellies wide and deep above their hips. Blood spilled out in a rush before their knees could buckle under them. Brown sludge from light breakfasts in anticipation of big Easter lunches ran forth from ruptured stomachs into the mixing life's blood on the sidewalks, curbs, and littered roads.

Others turned their backs to flee, but she stripped their Sunday best and striped their backs down to the bone. Most left the scene alive, but infection would take them slow and screaming in the coming days.

Mary reached the resting place, closed for Easter. No one is in the mood for a funeral on Easter. She lifted a boot and kicked the doors open against the natural turn of their hinges. The wood broke apart in ugly chucks, and she spread the splinters under her boots, marching over thick carpet through the dark halls.

The overripe floral smell of the viewing rooms gave way behind other flattened doors to the antiseptic smell of metal and tile in the real preparation areas beyond. She turned over tables and scattered wastes and other corpses that meant nothing to her.

She could smell her own. She could taste his presence behind the sanitized air.

Mary ripped the small square vault door off in one motion and rolled it across the floor like a stone or a severed head. She extended out the slab and cast aside the sheet covering his naked body.

"Come forth," she cried without looking at him, but nothing happened.

So, she looked.

He was beaten and bruised. Even the red clay couldn't hide that. He'd been striped by what may have been truck antennas. They must have really hated him to break their own trucks to beat him to death. The wounds had clotted and reopened more than once but finally stopped bleeding once he was dead.

They'd written on him in the clay and blood with all the grace and skill of toddlers fingerpainting in spilled shit. Slurs of all colors covered him along with accusations of Communist, Socialist, and Democrat.

His face was misshapen and disfigured, and his eyes sealed shut in puffy destruction.

What had they done to him beyond beat him and kill him? She didn't want to imagine but couldn't stop herself. Why hadn't they bothered to clean him yet?

"Come forth," she whispered.

One cord of muscle along one inner thigh twitched. She was sure she saw it. Mary cried the words over and over, echoing off the hard surfaces. Nothing else happened. Nothing came forth.

She kissed him all over his filthy body, his ruined face, his hard lips, but nothing else moved. She cursed him and slapped him, but nothing. She bit him in rage, tasting his cold spoiled flavor. She left her toothy crescent marks upon him, but nothing more.

The angel said she would know what to do, but she had no clue. Cupping one breast she worked the nipple between his stiff lips and teeth, trying to nurse him as she had done when they were both younger. She scraped herself on his upper teeth and shivered with a thrill of pain, but got no response from him.

Mary extracted herself from his mouth and fell on

him to weep. Her tears formed runnels through the matter stuck to his flesh. She smeared the words fingered upon his body, but none of it stuck to her immaculate skin.

She stood away from him and took up her whip. She lashed at him, adding to his wounds with dark postmortem ones of her own. If she could not raise him, she would tear him to pieces so she never had to look upon the evidence of his pain again.

The leather braid stroked his scrotum and jostled his limp penis. Her son's balls turned blue, then rose to a bruised purple, and finally warmed to an angry rashy red. Then, they swelled. His scrotum ballooned up, lost some of the wrinkles.

Where there was swelling, there was hope.

She reached out and cupped them. Warmth. Heat really. His balls were hot. Fluid sloshed around inside his scrotum under her massaging grip. The heat spread up from the base of his dead cock.

She still held onto to him as she swatted him with the handle of her whip.

"Come forth!" she shouted.

His body remained doll-still and cold, but his manhood rose from the dead. Rolling and twitching, his cock thickened in the middle, but the hardness evened out and it stood up straight and hot.

"Why won't you rise with it?"

The impressive erection lilted to one side. Lost a little of its stiffness.

She seized it and stroked it to return it to its full glory, hoping the new life and heat would spread. Mary gave a gentle kiss on the tip upon the ridge around the tip. "Please."

The cock throbbed in her fist. She waited for reaction from him and waited for the cock to erupt on its own. It started to wilt again. She stroked harder. Small abrasions started to form along the shaft from all the dry friction. Not knowing what that might do to his chances of resurrection, she leaned forward and pressed her lips to the head. She drooled over the cock, swirled her tongue around the head a few times, and slobbered some more. The saliva started to stroke its way under her fingers, until her hands moved slippery and fast up and down in a double fisted pump.

Her whip slithered into a coil on the floor.

Soon she felt like she was stroking a thing made of heated stone. Still, no signs of resurrection beyond his erection.

"I am the Redemptrix." She took a deep breath and sighed. "Where there is swelling, there is hope."

Reborn through the birth canal once more.

She climbed onto the table and straddled him. Mary rubbed herself against his girth until she inspired warm lubrication from herself. Raising up on her haunches, she inserted the dead man's cock inch by inch.

She slid up and down its length until her muscles fell into a rhythm perfected from much practice with less-deserving living men. As the conflicted pleasure of it pulsed through her body, a twisted vein stood out from her forehead. Still nothing from him.

Mary pumped harder until her ass slapped against his hot balls and his frigid thighs.

The ceiling cracked above her head, and the building folded away around her into two mounds of disaster. Cold Easter air and warm sunlight caressed her back, which glistened with a lather of sweat.

It had to mean something, so she fucked harder.

Vines climbed the walls of the empty churches around her. There were more such places than the town's sinful population could fill. The greenery dug its roots and feelers into corpses littering the street in her wake. Feeding upon some of the same dead who likely killed her son now under her, the vines crawled across the shingles and up the steeples, where they flowered in all the colors of infection.

Flowers covered the high crosses and hid them from view. They bushed out in an unruly tangle of petals and leaves.

Mary heaved for breath and switched up her pattern. She ground into his hips, arching her back to roll against him and take his full length in deep. Her knees flapped in a butterfly motion as she rubbed herself against him and stroked his cock in and out of her with each close thrust.

Mary showed her teeth. "Wake up!"

She pinched her own nipples hard enough to leave a mark and then pinched his too, pulling at the waxy flesh of his chest as she continued to ride him. Her pinches brought no flush of life to his flesh

In the distance, in towns across the country, people rose up from family tables smelling sex and salvation upon the air. Some slipped away in couples or occasional trios to have a romp of their own in celebration of life. Many husbands wanted it to be two women but settled for another dude in the mix, figuring they could sneak some anal out of the deal.

Others took the passion of the Redemptrix from

the air like an invisible electricity. The purification from her act of sacrifice inspired them to vote for lower taxes, less regulation, and the tastier of two unholinesses upon the ballot.

She felt the cock inside her pulse and swell tighter against her walls. The tighter grip pulled her along his discolored length like a sleeve before sliding him back inside to be born again. This might be it—her only chance. She bent his legs up into his chest and braced her legs on the slab for leverage as she fucked him amazon style. His whole body shook with each slapping impact. Flaps of loose flesh in early stages of decay fell away from his bones.

The unprocessed contents of his stomach and bowels shifted as she pressed into him. He let out a long, wet fart that left her thighs cold as she took all he had to offer inside her and back out again.

She had smelled worse from the living. Once when she was down blowing some trucker her cousin knew, he farted pure sulfur death into her face.

Her son's dead fart had a rotten sweet smell with woody accents and a citrus acidic reek like vinegar mixed with lemon. As it spread through the air before the breeze could waft it away, it took on other tones with almost a medicinal stench. It ranged from bitter and astringent to warm and sweet, but she was focused on other things, and it wasn't going well as she watched the corpse come apart under her instead of healing.

She refused to give up hope.

The righteous across the lower forty-eight cast aside their masks and showed their true faces to God and man. They tore their hearts asunder, and with the two halves, they could indulge the carnal and crucify a prophet on a Friday but be ready to seek forgiveness by Sunday and turn a profit on Monday. They were ready to answer the call to claim dominion over the world in God's name and in their own image of Him.

His holy balls tightened, and his dead cock throbbed visibly when she pulled up high enough on his shaft to show the action. A solid lump of something shot up inside her like a bullet. In death, his last bit of seminal fluid had turned inky black. The stuff was tacky like tar and tree resin dried hard and stiff.

She tried to keep going, but felt him quickly shrinking out of her. Mary spun about to work him with her mouth, where he was still creamy from being inside her. His scrotum cracked in multiple places and leaked clear, syrupy fluid across the slab. Pieces of his crumbling flesh floated in the stuff. Before she could work any more magic, his cock turned to dust with the rest of him. What didn't stick to the table blew away upon the wind.

She stood naked and exposed in the field that used to be a town. A place like Scully wouldn't be missed, and people driving through past the boarded-up businesses wouldn't notice the difference as the last few people slowly died inside their homes.

Flushed with an effort that felt like a failure, she scented their worship traveling back to her on the air like the fruity stench of a dead man's fart. They exalted her for what they thought she was and what they imagined she could do for them. And they imprinted their desires, fears, and prejudices upon him, the one their sin had killed. They imagined his face on every man they voted for to lead them to salvation in four-year cycles of redemption, disappointment, and the promise of rebirth. Like everything else, they shaped him in their minds into what they needed him to be.

"Then fucked that image into dust," the Redemptrix growled.

The grass turned yellow and exposed the dry dirt beneath as far as her voice carried.

She looked down at the great whip in her grasp and couldn't remember if she had held onto the thing the entire time she'd fucked him, but it was all she had to hold onto now.

Picking a direction, she set out. She would eventually find another town in another state that wouldn't be missed. She would insert herself into their polite company and show them who she really was. Break their hearts. Show them the cost of redemption and bring them to pay it.

TRUSTS AND ESTATES

HADLEY SCHERZ-SCHINDLER

*T*HE *PEOPLE WHO* came to Stinson James had
nowhere else to go. Stinson was the designated
child in his family who had to take on the mantle of
intermediary with darkness. His family had lived in
Charlottesville, Virginia, since it was founded in 1762.
They had come down from the Commonwealth of
Massachusetts not long before then. In the
Massachusetts Bay Colony, one of Stinson's ancestors
had made a deal with the dark side, ensuring that her
descendants would be successful and prosperous. Old
Lavinia James escaped being hanged for witchcraft in
Salem because her husband heard the rumblings
among the townsfolk and had the foresight to move
the family South in 1691. Deep in the Blue Ridge
Mountains was the perfect place to cultivate the
fertility of darkness.

Stinson helped some people realize their wildest
hopes and dreams. He rescued others from the
deepest pits of despair. The people who came to him
heard about him in cryptic discussions on the dark
web or by word of mouth from people at whiskey-

fueled late night poker games. They were never people Stinson knew in his daily life. Marcus Osgood was in the worst trouble in his life when he came to see Stinson. They met in Stinson's well-appointed office in a historic building in downtown Charlottesville. It was a late January afternoon, so the sky was already dark. Stinson had let his secretary go home for the day after she welcomed Mr. Osgood and showed him into Stinson's office. Marcus Osgood was a tall, handsome man in his late forties. He had a full head of wavy black hair, the athletic body of a tennis and squash player, and a warm, easygoing smile. He wore a bespoke suit under his grey herringbone wool overcoat. His black wingtips were freshly shined. His silver cufflinks were engraved with his family crest.

"What can I do for you today?" asked Stinson in his slow southern drawl.

"I'm in trouble," said Marcus. "It's really bad. I'm about to lose everything. Bad investments, bad couple years for my business, bad business partners."

"Do they owe you any money?" asked Stinson.

"They do," said Marcus. "But they've filed for bankruptcy. All of their money is tied up in offshore accounts. One of them left the country. My wife doesn't know anything about this. I have two kids in college up in the Northeast. Their tuition is through the roof."

Stinson nodded. He sat back in his chair and let Marcus tell him all about what went wrong with his business, what he had originally planned for it to be.

"If you met all of your goals, were financially secure, and could realize life as you wanted it, how would that life look?" asked Stinson.

26

"I would be so wealthy that I'd never have to worry about a business failing," said Marcus. "I'd be able to keep my house in Aspen and get an apartment in New York. My kids would be successful, I could fund my wife's hobby business and get her off the ground, and I'd have a few perks that would make my load a little lighter."

"Perks?" asked Stinson.

"You know what I mean." Marcus winked.

Stinson did not know exactly what he meant, but he had an idea.

"I can set this up for you," said Stinson. "But it's rather costly." Stinson rose and walked over to a credenza, where he poured both of them two fingers of Scotch. He handed the glass to Marcus.

"Anything," said Marcus. "I'd do almost anything to get myself out of this mess." He had looked up Stinson before he came to see him. He knew that Stinson James was a reputable attorney who represented some of the finest families in Virginia. He was not worried about getting entangled with a loan shark or some sleazeball who represented a crime syndicate, so when he volunteered to do anything, this was a well-considered risk.

"Would you sleep with a dead person?" asked Stinson a bit later, after Marcus had drunk a second pour of Scotch.

Marcus ran his hand through his thick black hair and laughed. "If it got me out of this mess, I sure would," said Marcus.

Stinson sat straight up in his chair, propped his elbows on his desk, and steepled his hands. "What I am about to propose to you may be rather odious when you first hear it. This offer needs to stay in this room, between us, or there will be rather unpleasant consequences. Do you understand?"

"Fully," said Marcus. "I know a gentleman's agreement and can fully abide by one."

"My family has been in the business of assisting people in need for a very, very long time," explained Stinson. "My father's line hails from Salem, Massachusetts. Those witch trials weren't just about blowing smoke. Those people who were executed had actual powers. My ancestors left Salem and moved to Virginia the year before the trials began. I can help you."

"How?" asked Marcus.

"Well, while I'll explain some of the particulars right now, maybe further on down the line, after a few years, I can do a better job of explaining the mechanics of it to you," said Stinson. "After you've seen the results, reaped the rewards, you're not going to really care about how it all actually works, though. I guarantee it."

"How much will it cost?" asked Marcus.

"That's the beauty of it," said Stinson. "I know you're in real trouble, so this is not going to require any sort of initial outlay. I am more of an intermediary in this situation ... Mr. Osgood, do you believe in God?"

Marcus smiled sheepishly. "Well, I go to Albemarle Presbyterian with my wife most Sunday mornings. We celebrate Christmas and Easter with gusto, but that's about as far as my religious observance stretches."

"Would you have any problem selling your soul to the devil?" asked Stinson.

Marcus laughed heartily. "I'm afraid I'm safely ensconced in the twenty-first century, Mr. Stinson. Sure, if you can broker that sale and I can get out of this financial mess, I'm all for it." Marcus thought Stinson James might be one card short of a full deck.

"Then I think I can help you," said Stinson. He took out a thick leather-bound ledger from the top drawer of his desk. "Two days from now, you will need to meet me here in Charlottesville at a designated spot to copulate with a recently deceased woman. She will be guaranteed to be free of all disease, of which I will provide you with documentation. You will be in a private room with her, which will be completely checked for any camera or audio recording devices. You will be required to climax to consummate this contract. Within a month of your performance, your financial worries will be mitigated. Increasingly, throughout that first year and then every year thereafter, the pleasures of your life will manifest magnificently. So, to reiterate, your only duties are the sex with a corpse and the pledge of your soul upon your death to the devil."

Marcus had been in a wild fraternity during college. This deal seemed like something his fraternity brothers may have cooked up. He figured he could get hammered enough to have sex with a dead body to have an amazing life. Especially if nobody would ever know about it.

"I will do this," said Marcus. "But if my financial position is not relieved and nothing much has happened within a few weeks, you will be hearing from me."

"Of course," said Stinson. He opened the ledger to

a fully drawn contract. "I will give you a copy of this agreement. Due to the unusual—somewhat occult—nature of the arrangement, I will need to prick your finger so as to dot your signature with blood."

Marcus laughed. "Okay, Mr. Warlock. Where do I sign?"

Stinson handed him a fountain pen and indicated the line at the bottom of the contract. "Go ahead and read it first," said Stinson. "Everything we discussed is laid out here."

"Okay," said Marcus. He skimmed the document and signed his name with a flourish.

Stinson took a diabetic testing kit out of a plastic wrapper as an easy, sanitary way to draw a drop of blood.

"Now, a bit of blood," he said as he pricked Marcus's finger and held it over the signature. The lights in the room flickered for a minute. "Very good." Stinson took a card from a drawer in his desk. "Here is the address of Caruthers Brothers Funeral Home. Meet me there at eleven p.m. two days from now. You may want to bring or be prepared to view on your phone something that will get you in the mood. If you need to drink during this adventure, I can give you a ride home and make sure your car ends up back at your house. I will bring a nice brandy."

The two men rose from their chairs and shook hands. "Mr. James," said Marcus.

"Call me Stinson," said Stinson.

"If you get me out of this mess," said Marcus, "I will be forever in your debt. Thank you for giving me some hope, however weird it is. As I said, you come highly recommended from a couple guys I trust very much, so I will see you in two days."

Stinson walked Marcus to the office door and locked it behind him. He went to his office bathroom to wash his hands. Even after two globs of soap, they still did not feel clean.

There was an ice storm the next day. Stinson wondered if the inclement weather would prevent Marcus from fulfilling his side of the bargain. Stinson was not a young man, but this was only the fifteenth person whom he had drawn into this sort of bargain. His Uncle Patrick had been so proud when he had handed over the reins of the business to Stinson. Stinson's father had passed away at a young age, and Uncle Patrick had no sons. There was no reason one of his daughters could not have fulfilled the role, but this was Charlottesville. It was much easier to be a white, Christian man in Charlottesville than a woman if one hoped to be successful in business. Stinson's wife, Mary Clementine, had no problem with Stinson working late. She had no idea what his work entailed, but it bought her and her children very nice things. The funeral home where Stinson was to meet Marcus was owned by one of his fraternity brothers from his years at the University of Virginia.

"Another one?" asked Matt Caruthers, proprietor of Caruthers Brothers Funeral Home.

"Yes," said Stinson. "Just like the November fifteenth situation. Whom do you have?"

Caruthers Brothers was the main funeral home for the whole surrounding area, so there was usually no shortage of dead people. Yet, one year, Stinson had to meet a client in the outskirts of D.C. because people had been unusually safe and healthy that year.

"I have just the body," said Matt Caruthers. "A university co-ed was in a fatal automobile collision in the ice storm. Sad affair—she was a pretty little thing."

"Is she very banged up?" asked Stinson.

"Not too bad," said Matt. "There were some facial lacerations and some broken ribs, but I can do wonders with her face. What else do you need?"

"Complete privacy," said Stinson. "Music. I'll bring a bottle of brandy and glassware. What's the lighting situation? If you could put something softer than that fluorescent, maybe a table lamp. I need it dim. The regular setup with the cot. Also, leave her naked, maybe with just a cloth draped across her. I have a feeling this fellow may get cold feet . . . although maybe not, with all his bravado."

"Will do," said Matt.

"Your compensation will be the same—twenty thousand cash," said Stinson. "I'll meet you at seven-thirty."

"Thank you, my friend," said Matt. "She'll be having a funeral mass early next week, so this mortal shell will be blessed before it is put into the ground." He said this more for himself than for Stinson. He believed that the girl's soul had already left her body, thus what he was doing was not really so wrong. He had to believe the corpses that came into his funeral home were just bodies, not people, or he would go mad.

The weather was better by the next day, so Stinson had no trouble getting to the funeral home, paying Matt, and then going out to dinner with one of his friends from law school in the interim. He had a couple martinis at dinner, so he was relaxed when he returned to the funeral home to wait for Marcus. There could be no mistake on his part. He used the key procured from Matt to let himself in by the back entrance. He went into the basement workroom to the wall of refrigerated drawers. The girl was in Drawer Three. Stinson pulled the drawer open and peeked under the cloth. She was beautiful—twenty-one years old, long blonde hair, buxom and soft, cold—but he could tell that Matt had already made up her face a bit. She had a bit of a glow even though the rest of her skin was a soft blue. Her eyes were closed as if she were sound asleep. She was perfect for his needs.

Stinson unscrewed the top of the brandy bottle he still had in his hand and took a long swig, then another. He needed to anoint her with the unholy oil. He set the bottle and a glass on a nearby tray. Then, he took a little round can for hair pomade out of his pocket. There was a Vaseline-like substance in it. His Uncle Patrick had given him twenty of these and told him where to procure more when he ran out. These were from a coven deep in the Appalachian Mountains. It was chrism, anti-blessed at a midnight, full moon ceremony of dark witches who dedicated their efforts to black magic. Stinson shuddered when he thought about its origins. He had to make an upside down cross on the girl's forehead with it and say, "Through this vessel, I offer you another, Dark Lord." Then, as had happened the last two times, and with just one more little swig of the brandy, Stinson explored the dead girl's body. He wiped the ointment on each of the nipples of her full breasts; he moved his fingers all around her nether regions, just playing, knowing that he could do what he wanted for fun without having to do any work to please her.

It sounded like a car door closed outside. He looked at his watch just to check and realized that he had only five minutes until Marcus was supposed to be there. Stinson rushed over to the sink to wash his hands and then went to wait by the back door.

"Good evening," he said to Marcus as he wiped his feet on the doormat.

"Hello," said Marcus. "Wow, it's cold out there. This is one of the worst Januarys that I can remember."

Stinson led Marcus down the basement hallway of the funeral home and into the employee lounge. "You can hang up your coat in here," said Stinson. He poured Marcus a snifter of brandy and handed him the drink. "You may need a little liquid courage. There's a little bit of soft music playing in there, the temperature in the room is a little colder than normal, and I have checked twice—no cameras, no microphones. You can lock the door from the inside." What Stinson did not tell him was that there was a one-way mirror high up on the wall where Stinson would be watching from the next room to ensure that the deal was consummated. "There is a large cot that has been set up. A table would be too high. You will need to help me move the body to the cot and off it back into storage."

Marcus was nodding as he drank.

"Would you like another?" asked Stinson.

"Yes, please," said Marcus. "I had one before I left the house. My wife thinks I'm at my usual Thursday night poker game. My poker buddies are not sure where I am. They know I took a huge hit financially, so they're not asking too many questions. I told them I may be at the game later tonight. It usually goes until two a.m."

This was unexpected. Usually, his clients were fairly shell-shocked after these encounters and needed to be driven home after the copious amounts of alcohol they had to consume. Stinson arched an eyebrow.

What he didn't know was that Marcus felt like he was accustomed to sleeping with the dead. His wife was as cold as any dead body. She had been a fun sorority girl when they dated in college, but she had hardened in the ensuing years. She had borne him the obligatory son and daughter but then demanded enough plastic surgery to return her stomach to its youthful flatness. No amount of Botox, though, could soften the hardness of the wealthy, entitled woman she had become. Priscilla Osgood had enrolled her children in Charlottesville's finest private schools so that their education was off of her hands. Those schools ensured enrollment at Ivy League colleges. Meanwhile, she spent her days playing tennis, taking tennis lessons, having after-tennis massages and rubdowns, and going to lunches and afternoon drinks with the other women with whom she played tennis. Every spring and fall, she went on a girls' week to a tropical tennis locale. She was ranked in her state master's circuit. Her diminutive stature made Marcus feel huge; her social ties had brought him much business, until his company took a nosedive, something of which Priscilla could never become aware. Even though he hated her as much as he loved her, it was as much for her that he was doing this as for himself.

"Let's do this, then," said Marcus. His phone was in the pocket of his blazer. He had already cued up some of his favorite porn in case he needed it. His goal was to be at the poker table with his buddies by twelve thirty at the latest.

"You can still back out of this before the actual consummation," said Stinson. He thought he may be missing something because the other men he had contracted with were usually nervous wrecks. Marcus was either a man without a conscience or hiding his misgivings very well. They walked down the hall to the workshop. Stinson pointed out the deadbolt lock on the door to Marcus as he shut the door behind them.

Marcus asked, "So, you haven't told me who I'd be fucking. Is it some old lady? It has to be a female. No way am I doing anything with a guy."

"No," said Stinson, pleased to finally see some normal interest. "You are a lucky man. A young college student was killed late last night in a car accident. She was very pretty and shapely. She awaits you in Drawer Three." Stinson pulled open the long drawer where the lovely corpse lay under the sheet.

"What's her name?" asked Marcus.

"Her name?" said Stinson. "I didn't even think to check. Are you sure you want to know?"

"Of course," said Marcus. "I always prided myself on calling out the right name whenever I was with someone."

Stinson looked at the paperwork affixed to the outside of the drawer. "Marla Straith."

"Hi, Marla," said Marcus as he pulled back the top of the sheet to look at her face.

Stinson looked at Marcus. He looked interested, not repulsed. They lifted the girl from the drawer to the stretcher and wheeled her over to a cot at the other side of the room. It was covered with a dark red velvet sheet. The overhead lighting was not on in this section, just a dim table lamp. They lifted the body off of the stretcher and placed her on top of the cot, still covered with a sheet.

"I'm going to need one more drink," said Marcus. "You can go."

"All right, then," said Stinson. "I'll be down in the employee lounge. Find me when you are finished and we'll move her back into storage. Remember, you must ejaculate. You can do this with or without a condom." He hated being so literal, but the terms had to be made clear.

"Right," said Marcus. "I'll see you later." He followed Stinson to the door and locked it behind him. *This is crazy*, he thought to himself. *Now I'm becoming like my grandmother, believing in all sorts of magic.* She was from the hills where magical things seemed to happen all the time.

Marcus prided himself on being able to perform anywhere at any time. He pulled the sheet off of the girl's face again. She was pretty. He wondered what her eyes looked like. They could be messed up from the accident, though. It would be better, he thought, to pretend like she was asleep.

He looked around the room. It was full of

machines and equipment to prepare bodies for their final rest. There was a curtain, like the kind in a hospital room, that could be drawn to separate the work side of the room from the side he was on with the cot. Marcus pulled the curtain closed. He started to take off his sweater and unbutton his shirt. He sat down and removed his shoes and socks. While he was sitting, he pulled up his favorite porn site on his phone to watch a couple minutes of something that would arouse him. Then, he completely removed the rest of his clothes and stood over the girl's body.

"Hi, Marla," he said. He downed the last sip of alcohol from his glass and stroked himself as he looked at her face. She was really pretty—high cheekbones, small nose, and full lips. He slowly pulled back the sheet. Her body was perfect, too—full, high breasts and tiny waist. He touched her everywhere. He had never been alone with a dead body before. Of course, he had attended many wakes where the bodies were at a distance and he was drinking and comforting the bereaved friend or relative. Here, though, he could do anything he wanted, even more so than with his wife.

Ugh, that was a stray thought. His would be the dead body if his wife ever found out about this. However, this was technically not cheating on her. Plus, he would probably be able to talk his way around this a lot better than the complete financial collapse that was about to take over their lives, that probably would still take over their lives—it was hard to believe that he was really doing anything other than having kinky sex that he could talk about with his friends many years hence.

He reached for the lubricant that Stinson had so courteously set on the table. He rubbed it generously up and down his shaft and forgot all about his wife as he looked at the young girl's beautiful body.

Marcus mounted her on the extra-wide cot. He gently separated her legs, felt around for ground zero, and guided himself inside of her. It was wonderfully tight in there. He wondered if she had been a virgin. "Marla, Marla, I wish you could enjoy this as much as I am," he said. He touched her breasts, but for himself. It was difficult to forget that he didn't have to bring her any pleasure. He moved back and forth quickly, his adrenaline spiked and negated any relaxing effects of all the alcohol he had ingested. He climaxed quickly with a loud groan.

In the next room, Stinson was disappointed that it was all over so quickly. He had taken his time stopping by the restroom, then pouring himself a drink before settling into a soft leather recliner behind the one-way mirror to watch Marcus. He was looking forward to pleasuring himself as he watched, but Marcus had finished just as Stinson was unzipping his own pants.

However, Marcus did not start getting dressed. He sat back from the girl, still in her, and started stroking her cold skin. He leaned over to lick her nipples. Then, he started sucking on her breast, and Stinson could tell he was getting excited again. Marcus would never know, but Stinson climaxed when Marcus did it the second time. Then, Marcus disengaged from the girl, but before he climbed completely off of her, he leaned forward and pushed back her left eyelid to see what color her eyes were.

"AAAAAAAAAAAAAAAAAAHHHHHHHHHHHH
HHHHHHHHHHHHHH," the bloodcurdling scream
echoed through the building.

Stinson slammed down the footrest of the recliner
and hurriedly zipped his pants and made himself
presentable. He could not see what Marcus saw. All
he saw was the naked Marcus leaning over the girl.
He took the time to lock the door behind him and
then started pounding on the door of the workshop.

"Marcus!" he said loudly but not shouting. If anyone
was walking by, they might call the police if they heard
screams in the funeral home in the middle of the night.
"Are you okay, man? Need help with anything?"

Marcus opened the door. He had tugged on his
underpants but was still unclothed otherwise. "She
looked at me," said Marcus. "I swear she could see
me."

"That's why I left her eyes closed," said Stinson.

"What?"

"I anointed her with some dark magical chrism
before you came," said Stinson. "As far as I know,
from what my ancestors told me and wrote about this
ritual, she could see you from the other side. Her eyes
are portals. Now, she knows who you are."

"Why didn't you tell me?" demanded Marcus as
he backed into the room and started putting on his
clothes.

"It wasn't relevant," said Stinson. "But now you
know. And now you've sealed the deal."

"It felt like a harmless prank in my mind since I
spoke with you a couple days ago," said Marcus as he
sat and tied his shoes. "It still did tonight, even when
I was going at it, but something about her eyes . . . "

Stinson was pulling the sheet up over the girl and pulling the stretcher back to the cot. "Let's put her back where she was. I need to return the room to working order. Why don't you have a seat." He brought over a thermos. "Here's some coffee I got earlier. Help yourself. Relax while I tidy up. I'm assuming you want a ride home or to the poker game?" Marcus had had a lot to drink just since he'd been there.

"Yes, thanks," he said. "I'd like to go home."

When Stinson drove his black Mercedes sedan around Marcus's circular drive in front of his house, he asked Marcus, "You read the copy of that contract that I sent home with you, right?" He had sent a redacted version of the contract that read more like a medical brochure home with Marcus when he had left his office days before.

"I did," said Marcus.

"You're going to sleep well tonight," said Stinson. "Don't be surprised when your life starts changing as early as tomorrow morning."

"I hope you're right," said Marcus. He was thoroughly spent and exhausted by this point. The ride home had calmed him. He tiptoed into his house and fell into bed already half asleep next to his wife. She scooted over a little in her sleep.

The next morning, Marcus did not have the hangover that he expected. His wife bustled into the room in her tiny tennis outfit.

"Are you sleeping in today?" she asked him.

"No, what time is it?" Marcus squinted at her.

"It's already nine o'clock," she said. "We have a court at the club at nine-thirty."

"We?" asked Marcus.

"Courtney, Meredith, Trin, and I," she said. "I'm about to leave."

"Wait," said Marcus. "Pris, come here for a second." He moved over to the middle of the bed and patted the mattress beside him.

His wife looked at him quizzically. Marcus was always a bear in the morning. They had a tacit agreement to not really talk until he had had at least two cups of coffee. Priscilla was always ready to charge forward the moment she woke. She walked over to the bed and sat down. Her tennis skirt barely covered her thighs. Her hair was in a high ponytail. She would have looked much younger than her forty-six years except for the sun damage on her cheeks. "What's up?" she asked. She was wearing the diamond tennis bracelet he had given her the previous Valentine's Day.

"I want to see you wearing nothing but that tennis bracelet," he growled as he stroked her arm.

"Marcus!" Priscilla protested. "It's morning. I just did my hair, and I'm about to walk out the door."

"I'll be quick," he promised as he stroked the top of her leg and then moved his fingers to stroke her inner thigh. "For a new pair of shoes, on my credit card?"

Priscilla smiled. "Well, Mr. Osgood, you just said the magic words that you know are sure to turn me on."

She stood and slid her skirt down her legs.

Priscilla still had the body of a cheerleader. Her spray-tanned legs were sinewy from her yoga classes. She smiled as she lifted her shirt over her head. Marcus propped himself up in bed. When she was completely naked, he beckoned her to join him. She crawled into bed. He pulled down the sheet to reveal that he was completely aroused, although this did more to impress him than her. He could tell that Priscilla was thinking about what shoes she was going to buy later. He pushed her back onto the bed and straddled her.

"Touch me," he ordered her. Priscilla licked the palm of her hand and stroked him. He smiled. "Actually, I'd like you to be on top."

"Marcus," protested Priscilla. "Can't you be on top this time?"

"For an unlimited shoe budget, I get to watch you," he said.

He rolled over onto his back. Priscilla dutifully mounted him. He started remembering how it felt to be inside Marla the night before, what she looked like, how she was a better version of Priscilla twenty-five years younger, while Priscilla, despite her protestations, was now very moist and slowly moving back and forth on top of him. He closed his eyes and thought of the girl in the funeral home and grew more and more excited.

Priscilla stopped moving.

Marcus was touching her breasts but realized they felt damp, slicker than just sweat. At that moment, he opened his eyes and saw blood dripping from her breasts, she was both urinating on him and losing control of her bowels. Everything was warm and wet and horrible. He sought her eyes and involuntarily clenched his bottom. There was petechial hemorrhaging—the whites of her eyes were completely red while she was staring off into the distance behind him.

"Priscilla! Priscilla!" he screamed. He pushed her off of him, and his penis was covered in a putrid, greenish vaginal discharge. The fluids kept leaking from her. He felt for a pulse in her neck. There was none as far as he could tell. He threw on a robe and dialed 911. He started administering CPR on her bloody chest when his cell phone buzzed. He answered on speaker in case it was the 911 operator.

"Marcus?" It was Stinson James.

"My wife is dying," said Marcus. "My wife is dying."

"She's already dead," said Stinson. "You can't mix the living and the dead."

"I'm doing CPR. I can't talk," replied Marcus breathlessly.

"Stop," said Stinson. "You can't revive her."

Marcus paused. "What do you mean?"

"Did you have sex with her without a condom?" asked Stinson.

"Yes," said Marcus. "We were in the middle of it when—"

"You did not read the fine print in the contract," said Stinson. "You can never again have bareback sex if you want the woman to live. You cannot mix the living and the dead."

The paramedics were pounding on Marcus' front door. One of them started to gag from the smell when Marcus led them into the bedroom. He realized part of the stench was coming from the putrid discharge and bodily fluids still covering him. They both choked back vomit when they saw Priscilla.

Towards the end of the wake several days later, at a different funeral home, Stinson James approached the semi-intoxicated Marcus Osgood when he was momentarily alone in front of the casket. Stinson stood next to him. "So, her family trust vested to you upon her death?"

"Yes," said Marcus.

"And I read in the paper that her shares in her college friend's startup vested as well," said Stinson.

"Yes," said Marcus. "I didn't realize she had those. I sold them back to her friend for two billion." Under his breath, Marcus asked, "So, I can never have unprotected sex again if I want the woman to live?"

"No," said Stinson.

"Why didn't you tell me?"

"It was in the contract," said Stinson. "You said you'd read it."

They stood side by side and gazed at Priscilla for another moment.

Marcus turned towards Stinson. "I don't want to see you again."

"You won't." After a beat he added, "But you'll be talking to my boss in the future."

EEVA

C.M. SAUNDERS

IT WAS JUST another Tuesday morning. I arrived
at work, made a coffee in the office kitchenette,
checked my email, replied to the most important
ones, had an impromptu staff meeting, got dragged
into a 25-minute conference call with a new client,
then checked my email again. All very mundane and
unremarkable. There was nothing weird about this
particular day at all. Things didn't get weird until I
found myself in a mid-morning lull and logged onto
Facebook.

There was a friend request. Nothing unusual
there. I get several a day. Mostly from obviously-fake
catfish accounts made in the image of busty Russian
beauties called Layla, or Filipino women who tell me
they love me then ask me to buy them a new phone.
Such is the lot of a single white dude on the internet.
This particular request, though, was different. I knew
her.

Eeva.

It had been fifteen years, but the resemblance was
unmistakable. The shoulder-length blonde hair, the

piercing blue eyes, the deathly-pale skin, the high cheek bones and tiny button nose. Time had been kind to her.

The moment I saw that face, the world around me melted away and I was drawn back to my halcyon student days.

I first met Eeva when we went to the same university in Southampton, a little city on the south coast of England whose claim to fame is being the place the Titanic sailed from. She had been standing in a corner of the student union nursing with what looked like a pint of cider and black, wearing faded ripped jeans and a black Alkaline Trio t-shirt. She was pretty, in a grungy, waif-like way. This might sound odd, but the thing that attracted me most was how vulnerable and out of place she looked. I sympathised because I spent the first half of my life being vulnerable and out of place. In fact, the feelings never really went away. I just got better at burying them.

Spurred on by my bullish and cocky uni mates, none of whom I stayed in contact with after we graduated, I puffed out my chest and strutted over. Making small talk was awkward at first, as it always is, but after a few minutes, the conversation started flowing. She told me her name was Eeva with two E's (how we laughed at that!) and she was an art student from Finland on an international exchange programme. Beyond being able to reel off the names of a few Premier League footballers, I knew nothing whatsoever about Finland. Still don't, to be honest.

Eeva and I exchanged phone numbers, and the night descended into the usual beer-soaked debauchery. I completely forgot about her until a few days later, when she sent me a text message inviting me over to her house for dinner. I gladly accepted. She lived just a mile or so from my student digs, and I walked there that very night, picking up a cheap bottle of red on the way, thinking that if she was from another country, she wouldn't know it only cost a fiver. All the way, I wondered what she looked like. I just couldn't remember. This was before the internet revolution meant you could just Google someone and find out more about them than you ever wanted to know.

The address she had given me wasn't hard to find. Just like she said, it was directly across the road from a little church. Heart thudding in my chest, I knocked on the door. Eeva answered immediately, looking resplendent in a dress so white it was hard to distinguish where her skin ended and the dress began. When she saw me, her face broke into a toothy smile, she came forward, stood on tip-toe, and kissed me on the cheek. She smelled musty. Damp, even. Not that I cared. That was how most students smelled. The night was off to a cracking start.

She took me by the hand and led me down a short, narrow passage which opened out into a large kitchen/dining room at the back of the house, complete with wooden table. Around the table were seated three other guys. That shocked me a little. What was the deal here? Were they her roommates? Or had she invited four guys on a group date? Was this how they did things in Finland?

Looking around at the other guys' faces, it was clear they didn't know what the fuck was going on either. All I could read was disappointment. And I knew how they felt. With every new dude that arrived, their chances of getting laid dropped in direct proportion. Assuming she wasn't into group sex, right now, there was a mere 25% chance of getting any action. On accepting Eeva's dinner invitation, we had undoubtedly all been under the impression that our chances had been substantially higher.

Trying to hide my confusion, I awkwardly greeted the other guys and took a seat at the table. Spaghetti Bolognese was on the menu. Along with cheese toasties and supermarket ready-meals, spag bol is a student standard. Unfortunately, Eeva's version was disgusting. The spaghetti was cold, and the minced meat off-coloured and streaky. I couldn't tell if it was pork or beef. A crimson fluid pooled on my plate. At first, I thought it was tomato juice, but I soon worked out that the mystery meat was virtually raw.

One of the three guys, who I was quickly coming to view as my competition for the evening after Eeva confessed both her housemates had gone out for the night, excused himself and left after just a couple of mouthfuls. That instantly boosted my chances to 33.3%. Something else that gave me a boost was the way Eeva flirted with me. Constantly making eyes and touching my arm. I'm not stupid. She flirted with the other guys too. But I was convinced she flirted with me more. Then again, maybe they all thought that, who knows? Your mind works in strange ways when beautiful girls are brought into the equation.

Even back then, I knew that in situations like that, it's often a case of sink or swim. You can be shy and retiring and let everyone else walk over you, or you can stamp your authority and make yourself the centre of attention. I played hard. And as the cheap wine flowed, my alpha male side came out. I was soon telling the group about the time I went to Ibiza and stayed up partying for four whole days, and the time I went to see Blink 182, sneaked backstage, and shared a spliff with Tom Delonge. This was pre-Enema of the State, so they were only playing local rock clubs, and in truth, it wasn't that difficult to get past security. In fact, there wasn't any, and I'm pretty sure Tom Delonge was glad of the free smoke.

Evidently not a fan, another the guys left midway through that story. And then there were three. It was touch and go with the last dude, a history student with glasses, called Daniel. It was clear Eeva was having great fun playing us off against each other, but some weirdly perverse part of me was actually enjoying the challenge.

It was nearing midnight by this point, and we'd drunk all the booze except half a bottle of Russian vodka Eeva had been keeping for a year. Nobody was brave enough to drink it, she said. We agreed to do shots, and that was the end of Daniel's night. After two, he threw up in the toilet and called a cab because he was too drunk to walk.

The moment Daniel was out of the door, I claimed my prize. I pushed Eeva against the wall, kissed her, and the next thing I knew, we were upstairs in her bedroom. The walls were painted red, and from the bay window, you could see the church across the road. Looking back, it all fit. But at the time, overcome with lust and longing and powered by red meat, machismo, and alcohol, I didn't care. All I cared about right then was Eeva.

I'd never had sex like that before in my life. It wasn't sensual, erotic, or tantalising, or any of that good romantic stuff. It was primal and animalistic. She snarled, grunted, and spat like a wild boar being fucked. She insisted on taking top position most of the time, which at first, I found a turn-on, along with the way she held my hands behind my head in a vice-like grip and licked my cheek. She could have done with a Freshmint, but I wasn't going to let a little thing like bad breath scupper my night.

Eeva thrust herself down on my cock so hard it actually hurt. When she came, she thrashed around on top of me like a wild thing, yelping and screeching as our pelvic bones were rammed painfully together time and time again.

When we finished, we both collapsed into the bed exhausted and drenched with sweat. I was asleep within minutes.

Some time later, I was awoken.

What was that?

Eeva was gone. I was alone in the bed, and I had a raging thirst. I assumed she must be in the toilet. Not knowing where the light switches were, I crept out of the bedroom and along the landing naked and in almost complete darkness. The bathroom was empty, the door standing open. I relieved myself, drank my fill from the cold tap, and made my way back to Eeva's bedroom. The house was deathly quiet. Nothing stirred.

Where could she be?

Inside the bedroom, something beckoned me to the bay window. I went over, cracked the curtains, and peered through the glass. Opposite the house, the church stood tall and proud, bathed in ethereal moonlight. I noticed for the first time that adjacent to the church was a small graveyard, the headstones sticking out of the ground like rotten teeth.

Something was moving in there.

I squinted and moved closer, my nose almost touching the glass. There was the unmistakable form of a human figure, almost translucent, gliding amongst the headstones. Convinced I was seeing a ghost, my heart leaped into my throat and stayed there, throbbing uncomfortably.

Then the realization hit me.

It wasn't a ghost.

It was Eeva.

What the fuck was she doing?

I knew art students could be an eccentric bunch, but this was taking it to the next level. Was she sleepwalking?

For a few moments, I stood still and contemplated what to do next. The situation was so bizarre, I had never experienced anything remotely like it and had no precedent on which to base my decisions. As I watched Eeva flit out of sight, my initial reaction was one of bafflement. Then I realised I was shivering. It was freezing. My next ex-girlfriend was out there alone in the middle of the night, naked or as good as naked. Anything could happen to her. My conscience demanded that I at least go and see what she was doing.

I quickly threw on my jeans, t-shirt, and trainers and dashed down the stairs, leaving the front door ajar because I didn't know where the key was. I ran across the road and up to the front of the church. It was locked and secured. The graveyard was surrounded by an ornately-designed wrought iron fence. It looked impenetrable, but moving along a few yards, I came across a gate for visitors. As quietly as I could, I opened it and stepped through. Beyond lay a path, flanked by bushes and wooden benches. This was where I'd seen Eeva from the window. Swallowing hard, I started down the path.

A silvery mist clung to the ground and swirled among the headstones, making the whole experience even more surreal than it already was. It was like being in a bad horror movie. As I ventured deeper into the graveyard, past an ornamental fish pond, the path took a soft right turn behind the church. There, it opened out into an area previously hidden by the huge gothic structure.

There was no sign of Eeva.

As I slowly walked the path, my eyes scanned the headstones on either side. I was surprised to find they weren't all old and crumbling. In this section, most looked shiny and new, the polished marble reflecting the moonlight. Some were still decorated with wreaths of fresh flowers. The graveyard must have recently been extended to include some new plots, I surmised. The only certainty in life is death, and there simply wasn't enough room in the ground for everyone.

I was wondering if I should call Eeva's name when I saw her again. She was kneeling on the ground in the shadow of a large yew tree, next to a grave. Her back was to me, so she didn't see me approaching. I stopped, transfixed.

What the fuck was she doing?

It looked like she was scrambling around on the ground next to a pile of soil and debris. My instinct told me to run. Get away from there. But in spite of myself, I took a few steps closer, squinting to see more. I couldn't tear my eyes away. It was like being stuck in a dream.

She wasn't scrambling, she was . . . digging.

With her bare hands.

She was completely naked, her skinny bone-white limbs now caked with dirt from the grave she was desecrating. Her arms moved piston-like with unnatural speed and dexterity, and all I could hear were the sounds of displaced soil and her grunts of exertion.

How could she have dug out so much soil without the aid of any tools in the few short minutes she had been here?

The moment it entered my head, the question sank to take its place with the plethora of others, many of which were far more pressing.

I remained frozen to the spot as, with feline agility, Eeva jumped into the open grave she had just excavated, landing atop what I assumed was a coffin with a thud. The hole wasn't deep enough to cover her entire body, but she immediately ducked out of view, which led me to assume she must be crouching down inside for some reason. The next thing I heard was the sound of splintering wood.

What the fuck?

She didn't come back up. The seconds crawled by. The fascination soon wore off, and I began to grow anxious. I had no idea what was going on but had come to the conclusion that whatever it was, it was illegal. At this point, I was still concerned with her safety more than anything else and running various scenarios through my mind. I still favoured my sleepwalking hypothesis but briefly entertained a succession of increasingly unlikely and outlandish theories. She was suffering a mental breakdown, she was some kind of Burke and Hare-style graverobber, or maybe she was looking for something she'd lost on a previous visit to the cemetery.

Anyway, it was time to call a halt to proceedings. I was cold and terrified someone was going to call the police.

I found myself edging forward, step by hesitant step.

As I drew nearer the open grave, I began to distinguish other noises coming from within. It wasn't the sound of digging anymore. Now, I could hear ripping, tearing, crunching, and slurping. The sounds made my stomach flip over.

I was just a couple of yards away when suddenly, Eeva's head and torso popped up. This time she was directly facing me, and our eyes locked. Her lower face and chest were smeared with dirt. It looked like she was drooling, and she was holding something in her filthy hands. It was a leg. A severed leg. Or, more accurately, a leg she had just ripped off the corpse in the ground. I was close enough to see that most of the meat on the calf had been gnawed away in chunks, and Eeva was still eating it. There was no blood, the blood having been replaced with embalming fluid.

When she saw me, she stopped chewing, but her eyes betrayed her feelings. There was no fear, guilt, or shame. Instead, she had the look of a child who had just been caught with their hand in the cookie jar. Mischievous, but simple and innocent. As the awful implications of what she was doing dawned on me, the blood in my veins turned to ice. I had to get away from there.

I turned and fled, bounding through the deserted graveyard as quickly as I could. I didn't go back to Eeva's house. I ran straight past and kept on running until I arrived home. Then, I locked the door and hid in my bedroom. I couldn't stop thinking about what I saw for weeks afterwards, or how that meat in the spaghetti Bolognese had tasted.

I never saw Eeva again, which was weird in itself. We attended the same uni, and Southampton is a small city. Yet I'd thought about that night often. At the time, it had been shocking to witness, yes. But over time, the disgust subsided, and I began to realize how invigorating and life-affirming the experience had been. The brutal sex, the adrenaline rush of doing something outside the law, seeing something I had never seen before. I had felt alive. Truly alive.

In the years since, my spirit had been crushed. I'd been stuffed in a corporate box, and now my sole reason for existing was to make money for fat men in suits who didn't even know my name. I couldn't remember the last time I got excited about anything.

I licked my lips to moisten them, then hit ACCEPT REQUEST.

Let the fun begin.

LET'S CUT UP DAD!

DOUGLAS FORD

*B*Y NOW, YOU'VE heard the stories from around here about people dying on their feet. "A Strange Phenomena," the headlines called it. Like Burl Malloy, who died while standing in line at the post office. Not even falling over like you'd expect. Not even having the decency to close his eyes. The line behind him kept growing, everyone too polite to ask him to move up, so it took a moment to figure out that it was a dead man holding everyone up at the post office. Or Milton Crow, who died pretty much the same way in the produce aisle of the local supermarket, though I don't think he inconvenienced anyone quite the same way as Burl Malloy. Plus a few others, all within a few weeks of one another, in a small area of the country. What you probably didn't hear about happened at my house.

By the time Dad died standing up, most of the other ones had already happened. People still don't know why. Just natural causes, supposedly. People do die, after all, and according to my biology teacher (he calls himself a scientist, but he just teaches, so judge

59

for yourself), it happens: people can die on their feet without falling over. It happened one time in a mall in China or Hong Kong or somewhere like that. But more than one in such a short span of time? In such a small area? It makes you wonder about asbestos or a mad scientist poisoning the water supply.

I found Dad first and initially didn't notice anything wrong. I didn't even know what killed him. He just stood there at our kitchen counter, the side with the burned Formica, thanks to my sister Eunice putting a red-hot frying pan on top of it. She didn't know better on account of being just a kid, but Dad hauled off and smacked her anyway. When I got in his face, telling him not to do that, because sisters stand up for each other, he picked up the frying pan and used it to hit me back. I still have a burn mark on my cheek from the hot side of that pan thanks to that. I didn't even cry, and I sure as hell didn't turn the other cheek.

Pretty much at that exact spot, and without any visible marks to explain how it happened, Dad died.

Seeing his eyes all open and glassy, I figured he was lost in thought.

But then I wondered how a man who never had a worthwhile thought in his life could suddenly find himself lost in one.

"Dad!" I snapped my fingers in his face. I clapped my hands. No reaction at all.

By this time, I'd already heard about Burl Malloy and the others, so it took me a moment, but I eventually deduced the situation I faced. I didn't even bother checking his pulse. Instead, I went to get Eunice out of Mom's room. Mom hardly ever left that room and slept there by herself.

I found Eunice doing what I expected to find her doing: rubbing Mom's bloated, purple ankles, trying to help her get some circulation going. Mom wanted Eunice to do this because Eunice, despite being younger than me, had big, meaty hands, and Mom claimed that only constant massaging would allow her any hope of eventually getting up and about on her own, perhaps one day becoming a productive member of society. Those bloated ankles, an unmistakable sign of terrible hypertension, meant that walking posed an imminent danger for Mom. Even thinking about walking could result in death by heart attack, so Mom stayed in bed all the time.

I told Eunice she needed to stop massaging and come with me. Mom grumbled when Eunice stopped rubbing, but I kissed her forehead and promised to bring her right back.

Eunice shook her wrists as she followed me down the hallway.

"What's wrong?" she asked.

I indicated her wrists. "I was going to ask you the same thing."

"Going numb," she said.

I said, "You won't believe this."

"It can be anything," said Eunice. "I literally don't care. I need a break. Mom's ankles aren't getting any better. No matter how hard I rub."

Eunice stopped complaining when I showed her Dad standing at the Formica counter. She knew at once he was dead. I find it kind of curious that she discerned the situation so quickly. It had taken me a moment to work it out, but Eunice began sobbing immediately. "No, no, no, no, no," she said, folding her hands under her chin, no longer caring one iota about her wrists. She made for the body like she intended to embrace it, but she also acted like the sight of it revolted her, so she kind of danced around it like she couldn't figure out what to do.

In truth, I almost wished she had hugged the body, just so I could see if this instant rigor mortis would hold up to Eunice pawing it. Would the body fall over? Or would the hand placed on the counter, right atop the burn mark, keep it anchored somehow?

"What do we do now?" Eunice asked after she finally stopped dancing around.

People always expect big sisters to have all the answers. People expect us to take charge. I might make a mistake now and then, but I wouldn't let Eunice down. "I only know one thing," I said. "If we're not careful, we're fucked." I pointed to the stale crackers on the counter, the moldy bread, the open container of spreadable butter. Maybe Dad planned to make himself a sandwich before he kicked it. "Who's paying for food now?"

Eunice looked around the kitchen as if an answer would magically present itself. "Mom?"

"Mom can't work," I said. "Her ankles, remember? Her hypertension? Just the thought of leaving that bed would make her blood pressure skyrocket. With her gone, we'd be orphans. Me, I'd be fine. I'm almost done with school. I'll be out in no time. Then it's off to the F. B. I. Academy for me. Soon enough, I'd have a job that earns me enough money so that I can fix this." I indicated the ugly burn mark on my face, practically a twin of that spot on the Formica. "But you? Just a kid and not right in the head. They'll put you in the funny farm. You want to go to the funny farm?"

Eunice did not want to go to the funny farm.

By that point, Mom started yelling for Eunice to get back to her and her ankles.

"You better get back at it. I'll think of a plan. And quit that crying," I said.

She made a poor attempt, but once she started massaging those big, purple ankles again, Mom wouldn't notice. If she did, I'd go in there with my ear buds and let Mom listen to the latest additions to my playlist, like some old songs by Iron Maiden I fell in love with recently, especially the songs on *Number of the Beast*. Mom would bob her head as she listened and not give Eunice's mewling any thought at all.

Meanwhile, I gave Dad's body another look. As a future F. B. I. agent, maybe I could use this situation to my advantage and gain some first-hand knowledge of what happens to a dead body. Last week, in biology class, I wanted to do a research paper on what happens to a dead body as it decomposes, but my teacher—a real stick in the mud—told me I needed to stick to his curriculum. He didn't even listen to my reasoning about how my project could turn into some useful career knowledge with the F. B. I. Now, I got to thinking about how one day I might get to investigate real life cases of people who died standing up, maybe eventually track down a mad scientist working for Russia or something.

A big carving knife sat near the moldy bread, giving me an idea.

I picked it up, feeling its weight. I tested its sharpness with the tip of my finger—just a little bit, a tiny prick, just enough to judge it plenty sharp. Unlike Eunice, I didn't like to cut myself. A tiny bead of blood told me all I needed to know.

Then I took the knife and slid the blade across the top of Dad's hand, the one he used to swing the frying pan at my face.

The blade opened up a slit in the hand, and dark red blood flowed for a moment, but not long.

Interesting.

It occurred to me that maybe I should write down the observations I made. I put down the knife and walked to the room I shared with Eunice, passing the open doorway to the one that Mom slept in by herself. I spied Eunice at the end of the bed, rubbing those ankles. She shot me a worried look.

To keep Mom from sensing anything wrong, I said, "Mom, you doing okay? Feeling better today?"

Mom said, "Your sister needs to rub harder."

"Eunice," I said, "rub harder."

Eunice glared at me but did as commanded.

I got a notebook and a pencil from my stuff and went back to the kitchen. Then I noted the time and my observation about the slit in the hand and how long it bled. I also recorded how the blood began to coagulate—or at least I think that's the word for when it started to turn brown.

Then I got curious about another thing. What would happen if I cut off a finger? Would a knife like the one I just used also cut through bone? As a future F. B. I. agent, I ought to know such things.

I reached for a cutting board, but not a wooden one. You shouldn't use a wooden cutting board when you cut meat on account of contamination sinking into the fine grains of the wood. Always use plastic for meat.

Then I had another thought. If I moved the hand to the cutting board, that might cause the whole body to topple over. I didn't want that to happen. One of the things I wanted to learn was how long the body would keep standing on its own after death.

I decided to leave the hand where it lay. Besides, after Eunice's hot pan, no point in worrying about a little more damage to the Formica. Not like a little blood and some knife marks would make it look worse. I placed the blade of the knife against the index finger, but paused to consider something else. I ought to try the thumb instead. When Dad leaned against the counter, he had that particular digit splayed pretty good.

I pressed down on the thumb with all my might, and at first, it wouldn't go through the bone. I tried sawing, but that didn't do any good.

Very interesting.

Remember, I did all this so that I could become a world-class F. B. I. agent someday.

Then it hit me: a hammer! I left the knife embedded in the thumb and grabbed one from the toolbox in the garage. Then I used the hammer to give two good whacks to the dull end of the blade, and on the second whack, it went all the way through. The thumb popped off. It lay there on the Formica in a pool of dark red.

I watched to see if the missing thumb would throw the body off balance and cause it to fall over.

I didn't want that to happen. I really wanted to learn how long a dead body would stay on its feet. To my delight, it didn't even wobble. Dad's dilated eyes stared ahead, unblinking.

What a great paper I could write for biology if that bonehead teacher would just let me.

I started doing more things after that. What else did I have to do on a Sunday? Sit in my bedroom and act bored?

Eunice came into the kitchen, rubbing her wrists as usual, just in time to see me getting to work on cutting off the whole hand.

After my experience with just a stupid thumb, I got smart with this one. In the back of the knife drawer, I found a big bread knife with a toothy, serrated blade. Using plenty of elbow grease, I'd made it more than halfway through flesh and bone when Eunice saw what I'd done and started screaming.

I had to throw Dad's thumb at her to make her stop.

"You cut off his finger!" Eunice wailed.

"That's a thumb," I said.

More wailing.

"You need to hush," I said. "What's Mom going to think?"

"I'm going to show her what you did." But Eunice just stared at the thumb on the linoleum. I knew she wouldn't. She wouldn't even bring herself to pick it up.

"Remember," I said, "you'll go to the funny farm."

She kept staring at the thumb, so I went back to my sawing. Plenty of blood got on the counter. Later,

I'd clean up what I could, but at this point, I didn't care about the mess.

When I finally cut through the hand, I felt an amazing sense of accomplishment. I pushed it away with the blade of the knife and stepped back to see what the body would do. I didn't even breathe, anxious to see if it would fall.

Once more, amazingly, it didn't even totter.

"Now that's very interesting," I said out loud.

Cautiously, Eunice stepped closer, curious in spite of herself to see what I found so fascinating. Her lips curled in disgust when she saw that I cut off the hand, but I'll hand it to Eunice (ha!): she didn't start wailing again.

"You see that? He's still standing up. I thought for sure that without the hand propping him up he'd topple over." Enjoying how Eunice looked over my shoulder, I wrote this observation in my notebook. Blotches of blood smeared the page, but I couldn't help it.

I turned toward her, tapping the eraser side of the pencil against my chin, imitating the thoughtful look my biology teacher would give me when I asked him to curve a grade.

"Eunice, do you know what rigor mortis is?"

She nodded, but I know she didn't.

"Everything stiffens when you die," I said. "Your whole body. I think rigor mortis might keep Dad standing forever."

Eunice nodded. I kept tapping the pencil as I spoke.

"Like, what would happen if I sawed off the whole arm? You'd think that might shift all the weight to the other side and then he'd fall over for sure. But then again . . . " I really wanted to try it, but I didn't know if I could pull it off with kitchen knives.

Then Eunice said something that made me want to hug and kiss her.

"Or his leg," she said. "He couldn't stand on just one, could he?"

Even a crazy head like her can say something profound once in a while.

"Indeed," I said. "Interesting."

Later, I stood outside the house smoking a cigarette, thinking. Eunice had to stay inside to do more ankle rubbing and, later on, fix Mom some dinner. Other than going to the bathroom, which she needed Eunice's help to do (and frankly, she did that in bed sometimes), Mom didn't really ever leave her bedroom. That gave me some alone time to do my thinking and to smoke the cigarette I got from Jace Armstrong in exchange for rubbing his thing behind the football stadium. I did that fairly regularly because I needed a smoke once in a while, and besides, I like seeing how the milk comes out of boys. Jace Armstrong sometimes asked me to let him put his thing somewhere other than my hand, but I'd always tell him no way. I just needed a couple of smokes. Jace wanted me to do it with my head turned to the side so he couldn't see the mark left by the frying pan, but I refused. If he wanted me to help him get the milk out, he'd have to see my whole face.

Smoking, I dreamed of the day that they'd call me in as an ace F. B. I. agent to figure out the mystery of why people died standing up. What I did now would help that day come true.

I thought about what Eunice said about the leg, and now, I really wanted to try that. Ideas started forming.

Later, after some quality time with Mom where I let her listen to more Iron Maiden, Eunice and I went to bed. We shared a bedroom and sometimes talked before passing out, but tonight, we stayed pretty quiet.

The quiet broke when Eunice asked me a question.

"What killed Dad? Why'd he die?"

I thought about that already. "Well, he drank a lot. He put butter on everything. He put butter on his butter. You've seen him do that, haven't you? Probably a heart attack. Plus, he had a stressful job."

Saying that reminded me of something important.

"Eunice," I said, "you can't go to school tomorrow."

"Why not?" Eunice actually liked school.

"Because someone needs to be home if the people at the water treatment plant call up and asks why Dad isn't at work. You can't let Mom answer the phone and find out he's not there. She'll get wise to what's going on."

In the dark, I could hear the gears turning in that crazy head of hers.

"How am I supposed to do that? I'll be rubbing ankles all day if I stay home. Please, Lou Ellen, I don't want to stay home."

"You can get up if the phone rings. It'll be for just a few days," I said.

"A few days? No!" That wailing started again.

I said, "I don't need to tell you about how what I'm

doing will have consequences for the future. When I'm in the F. B. I., I can use this experience to solve crimes. Also, the money will pay for my plastic surgery. You don't want me to have this ugly mark forever, do you?"

I could have reminded her that I got it by standing up for her. I didn't need to. She thought about it quietly.

"Do you?" I said again.

"No."

More quiet, until: "Lou Ellen, would a stressful job make Dad do other things?"

I bit my tongue before answering. "What other things?"

She acted like she didn't want to say it. I had a feeling I knew what she meant. Dad liked to hit both of us, me especially, but he considered Eunice his favorite and sometimes touched her in different ways, especially after Mom got laid up with her ankle problems.

"Just other things," she said.

"God's bones, Eunice, I cannot fathom the ways of fathers. Or mothers, for that matter." In truth, I didn't like to think about it. "Just go to sleep."

She must've tried because she got quiet, but after a bit, I started to hear a rustling sound.

"Eunice, are you cutting yourself again?" When she didn't answer, I knew she was; but after a while, I fell asleep, and I assume that so did she.

Eunice kept grumbling about it, but I convinced her to fake some coughs the next morning, and it didn't take many to convince Mom that Eunice needed to stay home.

Meanwhile, I woke up refreshed and with a new plan.

When I saw Jace Armstrong in the morning, I said, sure, I'd meet him behind the stadium, but instead of a cigarette, he had to bring me something else: an electric tool I could use for cutting, something tough, like a saw I could hold in one hand. He looked at me like I'd gone crazy, but I threatened not to show up as usual, so he said he'd see what he could do, mentioning something about the equipment in the shop classroom. Sure enough, he came through. When the milk came out of him, it looked a little bit yellow, so I thought it my duty to advise him to see a doctor or something to have it checked out. I took the small bag he brought me and left him to figure that out on his own.

Eunice met me in the kitchen when I came home. She looked worried.

"Dad's alive, I think."

I looked at the body. It still stood as I'd left it, the eyes starting to turn the same color I milked out of Jace Armstrong not long ago. The surrounding skin looked brownish and had developed an oily sheen.

"That's impossible," I said, but I felt a lump of worry growing in my throat. "Why are you saying that?"

"He farted. Twice."

That made me breathe a sigh of relief. "Dead bodies do that," I said. "Gas moves around them.

71

Things probably shifted a little, and he let one or two rip. That's all."

"It stank."

I sniffed the air. It still did, though some of the odor must've stemmed from the normal decomposition. I did detect a distinct odor in the air, something mixing with the fumes that clung to Dad from his job at the water treatment plant, a familiar farty smell, the kind that Dad's body used to let off after a big meal at KFC. Hopefully, I'd get to open up the stomach at some point. That oily sheen on his skin made me wonder what would happen if we put him into a giant fryer. Imagine the smells then.

"Besides," she said, still clinging to her illusions, "nothing shifted, right? He's still standing in the same place."

Good point. I needed to include the farting in my notes.

"You don't think," she said, "that he walked around last night, do you?"

Trying out my best F. B. I. impression, I said, "What evidence do you have?"

"Evidence?"

"You know, do you see any blood trailing down the hallway? A blotchy fingerprint anywhere?"

My sister stared at me. I did love her, I really did.

"Gadzooks, Eunice, you truly are destined for the funny farm. I'm trying to tell you that without evidence, we can conclude it didn't happen. The body's right where it's stood all along, which is truly a mystery unto itself. And it's one that I'm developing methods of solving." I started to pull my new cutting tool from the bag when a thought hit me. "Eunice, pull down your shorts."

"No. Why?"

"I want to see the tops of your legs. You were cutting yourself last night, weren't you?"

"No. I swear."

"I mean it, Eunice. I know how you get."

Again, she swore that she'd done nothing of the kind, but something about the way she looked at the body gave away what she'd done instead. Leaning over the Formica, I saw what she did to the arm above the stump.

Several cuts, nine or ten of them. And she went deep, too, deeper than she went on herself.

I didn't know whether to yell at Eunice or to congratulate myself on deducing what happened so quickly. F. B. I. Academy, watch out!

Deep breaths allowed me to calm down and not yell. At least Eunice finally stopped cutting herself. Of course, now that she got a taste of what it felt like to cut someone else then maybe she'd now set off on the path to becoming a psycho killer, one that I'd have to hunt down someday. Imagine how that would play in the news: Star F. B. I. agent with a miraculously repaired face has to hunt down and capture her own sister who went psycho. For Eunice's sake, I sincerely hoped that wouldn't happen. No way could she ever elude me.

She watched as I set out the saw that Jace gave me. It came with a long cord. As I talked to Eunice, I plugged it in to the kitchen socket. "You've got to promise me that you'll never, ever touch this body again. Treat it like you would evidence at a crime scene."

She nodded and said something I couldn't hear

because I pressed the saw's power button, letting out a shrill whine. That sound concerned me.

"What's Mom doing? Eating?" I asked.

Eunice shook her head. "Napping. I rubbed her ankles for hours."

"She might not sleep through this." Later, I decided; I'd use the saw later, when I could avoid waking Mom.

Inspiration for what to do in the meantime came from Eunice.

She said, "Cut off his legs so he can't walk down the hall and come into our room."

"He'd fall for sure if I did that, and what did I just tell you about evidence? He's deader than a doornail."

One look at Eunice's expression told me that I hadn't convinced her.

"I'll tell you what. There's something else I was thinking of trying. Let's say you're right and that Dad's really alive. Never mind the fact that I cut off his hand and he showed no reaction. Let's say he's just tricking us. He plans on waiting until we're asleep and then stalking us."

The look of fear on Eunice's face!

"I'm just saying 'what if.' He's not. But if he was, he'd need his eyes to see, right?"

Eunice looked a little more hopeful, but doubt still clouded her features. Nevertheless, she nodded.

"Well, I need to learn how hard it is to take out a human eye. What kind of tool a criminal might use. Mind you, I'm doing this to learn."

"For when you join the F. B. I."

"Exactly." I looked around the kitchen, not wanting to use a knife. For one thing, a knife might set a bad example for Eunice, and before I knew it, she'd go back to cutting the body the first moment I turned around. I picked up a spoon, but inspiration hit me when I saw a plastic bag with some left-over packets from K. F. C.

I picked up a spork, that spoony instrument with sharp points.

"Perfect," I said to Eunice.

Next, I got a chair to stand on. Even though I stood just about as tall as Dad, I figured a little more height would help me do what I planned.

Eunice watched as I stood on the chair with the spork. If I had sleeves, I'd have rolled them up. Gently, at first, I started digging around the edges of the left eye, so foggy and unseeing now that Eunice really had nothing to worry about. Anyone could see he was dead. I needed to not only dig but cut, digging through the spongy surface so that I could get behind the eye and pop it out in one piece.

It turned out that I didn't use a gentle enough touch. I punctured the eye, and it broke apart. Out came a clear fluid (not at all like the yellow milk that came out of Jace Armstrong. I do hope he sees a doctor.).

"Goddammit," I said. But my mom didn't raise a quitter, so as Eunice continued to watch, I started again on the right eye.

I did a lot better that time. Out popped the eye, dangling by a veiny cord. The optic nerve, of course. "Fascinating," I said to Eunice as we both regarded my work. Surprisingly, she no longer fussed about the messes I made and which I'd need to clean up later. "See, Eunice, even though I messed up that one eye, it's still helpful for me to know what it looks like when you bust up an eye with a spork. And I can also know," here, I picked up the dangling eye and let it fall back against the body's chin like a pendulum, "what an optic nerve looks like. I wonder how hard it is to cut it."

If Eunice impressed me before by not gagging at all the goo that came out of the left eye or the bloody glob that dangled like rotten fruit from the other eye socket, she really showed me something by going into a kitchen drawer and pulling forth our best pair of shears. She held them out for me to see.

"Can I try?" she said.

"Absolutely not. You're just a kid, and I'm afraid you might decide you enjoy that kind of thing. You might decide to grow up and become a psycho killer, and then the F. B. I. will send me on a manhunt after you. You don't want that to happen, do you?"

"No?" She said it like she was asking a question.

"Then give me those shears."

It turned out not too hard to cut the optic nerve. Kind of like cutting a thick, wet string. The eye fell to the floor with a plop, but the impact didn't bust it. I decided to put it in the lunchbox I kept under my bed, where I'd already stored the hand and the thumb.

Before I could do that, Eunice started jumping and yelling. "He is alive, he is, he is!"

I about had a heart attack myself as I turned in time to see that the body did, in fact, seem to lurch and sway a bit.

"You need to kill him, Lou Ellen! Please, please, please."

"You need to shut up before Mom hears you," I said, but too late.

Mom's voice came to us from the other room, asking what we'd gotten into and what exactly needed killing.

"Just a snake," I called back. "Crazy-head Eunice brought another snake into the house."

"You kill it right away, Lou Ellen. Cut off its head. Eunice! No more snakes in the house!"

Eunice started to shout that she'd done no such thing, but I gave her the stink-eye, and she closed her mouth real quick.

"He's not alive," I said to Eunice with my best indoor voice. "I just threw him off balance." Though I had to admit that it freaked me out just a bit to see the body move, but one of us needed to remain logical. The F. B. I. only wanted agents who could think logically.

Neither of us did so much as breathe as we watched to see if the body would finally topple. It looked likely to happen at any moment.

"I wonder if I could redistribute some weight on top," I said.

Of course, Eunice had no idea what I meant.

I said, "I'm thinking about cutting off the head. Or maybe just cut deep enough so that I can push it back down against his back. I still need to learn how long he can keep standing. For future investigations, of course."

Eunice said she understood, but I don't think she really did.

"Don't worry about what I'm going to do," I said. "You need to start rubbing Mom's ankles. Come with me."

On account of the noise I planned to make, I

needed something to preoccupy Mom, so I led Eunice back to her room. As she gripped Mom's swollen ankles (which looked more and more like purple hams to me), I put my earbuds in Mom's ears. I'd gotten tired of Iron Maiden, but I still acted excited about a song called "Can I Play with Madness." I set it on repeat and watched Mom's big head move along with the melody.

"You do have such interesting taste in music, Lou Ellen," said Mom. Her eyes closed, and once I heard the moans and knew that Eunice had begun rubbing to her satisfaction, I went back to the kitchen to do what I really looked forward to doing: sawing into the body's neck.

No more reason to worry about the blare of the power saw. It fit perfectly in my hand, and even if I didn't have Eunice's iron grip (which would one day make her a formidable psycho killer), I could still handle it pretty well. Getting back up on the chair, I took some of Dad's sparse hair in my hand to hold him steady. Then I placed the blade against his throat, just above the Adam's apple, and then I hit the power button.

As I suspected, I didn't have to worry about blood. By now, the blood had settled down low in his legs.

But I didn't anticipate the other thing. The gyrating blade sent wet chunks of decaying flesh flying everywhere, including the floor, the Formica, and even my face. So much got into my eyes that I could hardly see. Tiny bits got into my mouth too, and I accidentally swallowed them without thinking. They had the bitter taste of spoiled egg.

I kept at it, anyway, not even stopping when I got

to the hard bits. In the end, I had to hand it to Jace Armstrong (ha, there I go again)—he definitely came through and got me the right tool. Next time, when I finished him up and he asked if he could kiss the good side of my face, I just might let him. Usually, I would tell him he'd have to kiss both sides, but I felt something warm for him now.

Thanks to Jace Armstrong, I now know how long it takes to saw nearly all the way through someone's neck—fifteen minutes exactly, and that involves using a mechanical tool. Plus, I could now record in my notebook how messy the process turned out. When I saw myself in the bathroom mirror, I looked quite the fright, covered with wet yellow and gray chunks of meat, some of it even stuck in my hair. I opened my eyes wide and made silent screaming faces at myself in the mirror. I wouldn't want to face myself as an F. B. I. agent.

I cleaned myself up a little before Eunice could see me. When I came out of the shower, I started a load of laundry in the garage. In the kitchen, I found Eunice already done massaging ankles. She stared at what I'd done with the body.

I didn't cut all the head off all the way, just enough where I could force it back so that if it still had eyes that worked, those eyes would see whatever stood behind it upside down. A chunk of windpipe stuck up from the neck. When I pushed the head back, I actually heard a sigh come up from it, along with whiff of an old KFC meal. I'd make sure to record that observation in my notebook.

Eunice seemed mesmerized by the body's appearance, which I admit looked weird, and she didn't say anything.

"Notice it's not wobbling at all," I said. "Pushing the head back like that definitely distributed the weight better. It has a small head to go with that small brain, and without eyes, I'm sure it weighs even less, but that certainly did the trick. It'd probably stand on its own for a long time.

"Dad."

"What?"

"You keep saying it, but it's Dad," she said.

"It was once," I said. "Not anymore. He can't see or walk down the hall anymore, Eunice. He can't come in our room the way he used to." For some reason, it hurt a little to say this out loud.

She continued to stare at it, not even acknowledging what I just said.

"Eunice, I know you would always pretend to be asleep. I would too. I'm sorry I never opened my eyes and did anything. I'm sorry the only time I ever did anything was that time with the frying pan."

Still not looking at me, she said, "I don't think this'll stop him. He doesn't even want to fall down."

"We should go to bed early," I said. "Maybe you can go to school tomorrow. I'll tell Mom I'm sick and stay home. You can say you feel better."

"I don't," she said. "I don't feel better at all."

"Wait and see how you feel tomorrow."

That night, I had such a weird dream. I dreamed that they finally took Eunice to the funny farm, but before she left, she had a pet snake, just a tiny one, and even though I hate snakes, I promised her that I'd take care of it in her absence. And I tried so hard to love that snake the way Eunice did, but every time I picked it up, it bit me. Even worse, no matter how gently I tried to hold it, it fought me, and at one point, I accidentally broke the snake in half. In the dream, I thought I killed it, but the second segment of the body grew a new head, so I wound up with two angry snakes to contend with.

What an awful dream.

I might have welcomed something wakening me up from it.

Just not what actually did wake me.

A whirring sound. The electric saw that Jace Armstrong gave me, blaring through the dark house.

I looked over at Eunice's empty bed and knew in an instant something awful was happening.

And I didn't have earbuds in Mom's ears. I took them out before going to bed. She would hear.

I rushed into the kitchen, and you won't believe what I saw.

Eunice had managed to unbuckle the body's trousers, and they lay with its boxers in a heap around its ankles. Its head still leaned way back, and the body showed no signs of falling over.

I could almost feel pride in Eunice for managing this feat, except for what I caught her doing.

She was using the saw to cut off the thing that the milk comes out of. I mean the balls and the pecker itself.

I came in just in time to see the last piece of rotten flesh give way and the whole package fall in a lump between Eunice's knees.

She looked at me with a face as horrid as the one I saw in the mirror, all covered in sticky flesh.

"Now he can't do anything," she said. The grin she flashed me signaled the emergence of a master criminal, a formidable psycho.

I almost smiled back.

Except Mom chose this moment to finally walk out of her room, to test the ankles that we all knew could never hold her up. She hadn't walked in so long, and she'd put on the kind of weight that those ankles just couldn't handle. But I guess all that massaging had finally paid off. A miracle, I suppose. "A strange phenomenon," one might say.

"What on earth are you girls doing?" she said, bracing herself against the wall as she rounded the corner in heavy, lumbering steps.

Seeing mad Eunice covered in ruined flesh must've done it. That along with the fact that I never did such a good job of cleaning up the kitchen. Not to mention the body's head pressed down against its back, gazing back at Mom upside down.

Mom died on the spot.

A heart attack, most likely.

And here's the kicker: she died standing up too, even with those terrible ankles.

The mystery continued, and I had a lot of work to do in order to solve it.

Revenge! She Cried

Heinrich von Wolfcastle

BROWN LIQUID GATHERS as a small puddle where the edge of the ceiling meets the wall. It hovers there, tentatively poised, before gravity runs it down in streams between flakes of peeled paint. When the droplets reach the ground, they don't splatter but stretch and dissipate between cracks carved into the cement floor.

My breath returns in shambles at first—fragmented huffs of inhalations colliding with exhalations. I move my hand down the side of the bed to grip the metal frame with a groan—a sound, I realize, that I was already making. The bar is cold in my hand and wet with blood. I am wet with blood.

I notice that the hanging lightbulb makes a strange buzzing sound. A shadow wipes across a credenza and disappears as the current stabilizes. The credenza, like everything else in this house, leans forward, avoiding an uncomfortable fondling from the wall.

The bed is tilted too, and I feel its asymmetrical pull on my body when I rise. The floor is cold against my feet, scratchy in patches where my socks have worn away. As soon as I am vertical, I am hobbling to catch myself in the doorframe.

The walk from the room is long and meandering. The walls play with me, absorbing me and repelling me, before I arrive at the stairs, where reflections of broken glass glimmer and wince in the carpet. I move over them, each step placed intentionally to avoid their wrath.

My arrival from the basement is announced by the door's collision with the wall, but I am only met by curious silence. I labor forward, claiming a chef's knife from the kitchen counter on my trek towards finding him.

He is lying on the couch. His body is sprawled across the cushions, limp and depleted. But I notice a subtle rising and falling movement in his chest.

"Wake up," I command, but my voice is a meek whisper.

His chest continues to inflate and deflate.

"Wake up, motherfucker."

He stirs and moves his head to an angle where I can see his pulse faintly beating in his neck. There is blood caked into his beard stubble, but it does nothing to quell my rage.

"Wake up!" I scream. Blood spits forth from the froth on my lips. With trembling hands, I raise the knife and bring it down without pause.

His eyes open in disbelief as I submerge the blade into his gut. He lets out a sound—a pitying awww—as it enters his belly. His lips pucker, and for a moment, I almost think he wants to kiss me again.

"You stupid motherfucker," I hiss, locking my eyes

onto his. I want to hold his pain in my gaze, but it's fleeting, slipping away with each second, and I am losing him.

"No," I mutter. "Wait."

He leans forward to hang onto me but misses and crumples over himself in a heap.

"No," I say again. "You can't leave. Not yet—" But he is gone.

I pull the knife from his stomach and drop it on his back. My hands shake, and I watch them tremble, looking for them to naturally settle. But they cannot settle because I am not settled.

"That fucker," I pout to myself.

I drop onto the couch next to his corpse—the empty, hollow thing that should still be him, that should still be alive with agony.

"Fuck!" I scream. But no amount of screaming will bring him back to life. No amount of anything will bring him back to life, except, perhaps, the book.

I turn and find it resting nobly on the small table beside the couch. It looks at me and I look back at it, neither of us compromising our stare. Yet, its expression is smug, knowing I am already indebted to it.

Before I can pause to consider otherwise, I am thumbing through its leather pages. The binding is worn, and it spreads itself easily to the incantation I need, conveniently already earmarked by bloody fingerprints.

I reclaim the knife and carve it into his back with generous pressure. I move it like an artist's brush, painting deep, bloody valleys in his flesh.

The words I follow are foreign to me, and they

stagger awkwardly from my mouth in serrated starts and stops. But they work.

I sigh as I finish the spell, just as the book instructs. And though I cannot see it, I sense my breath travel an invisible thread from my body to his. It won't resuscitate him immediately. I know that. And I am OK with that because I am exhausted, and I can use a rest.

"You fucking bitch. You stupid fucking bitch!" he gargles.

His hands are wrapped around my neck, squeezing, pulsing with his anger.

"You brought me back? You think you're going to kill me again?" He presses down on me, putting his weight into his grip. "I brought you back, you bitch."

He stabs his finger at my mouth, digging his nail into my lips. I meet his gesture and snap at it, my teeth cutting into and breaking the tip of it from his hand.

"Ah, goddamn it!" he cries, and reaches back to strike my nose. I hear the crack of cartilage before I feel the dull ache that grows and swells over my face.

"Not smart to fall asleep, Alice! You should've learned from my mistakes!" He squeezes harder and the ceiling swirls.

My hands go up to meet his but fall back on my own face.

"Do you know what I sacrificed to bring you back? I lost a leg for you, you ungrateful cunt."

His words are excited but quiet.

"Hey! Don't you disappear on me," he instructs. "Don't you die on me—not yet." But he doesn't stop choking me. "Fuck."

And everything goes quiet.

My eyes open to a pool of brown liquid rot collecting in the corner of the room. It spills down the wall adjacent to me, its trails illuminated by the lightbulb dangling by frayed wires. I reach for the bedframe to find myself, hoping the feedback will help my brain dispel its dizziness before I place my foot on the floor, but my wrists are restrained by twine.

My breath returns in a stuttering shuffle. The air is cold and damp, and it feels good on the open wounds that cover my stomach and chest—cut, carved, and traced by blade at least twice over.

Something foreign sits against the inside of my cheek. I use my tongue to push it from my mouth and see the tip of his finger. I spit a combination of our blood after it. My face is stained by something once wet that cracks every time I grimace.

I wriggle my hands against the twine, secured to the bedframe. The twine is strong enough to hold me, but the rusted metal is decrepit enough to cut it. I work my hands back and forth, building friction against the twine, and it snaps even easier than I expect.

"Stupid asshole," I mutter.

I dangle my feet tentatively over the ground before I bear weight on them. My left leg feels vacant, like a reinflated balloon, and it collapses when I go to stand.

My crawl to the stairs is grueling and time consuming. When I get there, I find the strength to support myself with the help of the rail, but not before shards of glass are buried in the skin of my stomach, arms, and legs. I tread over their jagged edges using my left arm to hoist myself along the handrail—pulling myself forward and upward in caterpillar strides. The ascent up the stairs is no easier, and when I arrive to the door, I find it locked.

I rattle my shoulder against the door. The hinges on the frame are weak, but I am weaker. I lean forward, placing every ounce of weight in my withered body against it. Slowly, the wood in the frame begins to crack. The splintering sound drives my excitement, and I hold the door handle to support myself so that I can drive my shoulder into it. I do it again. And again. And again.

As the frame crumbles, I crumble with it, falling on top of the door as it slams into the ground. The sound is loud enough to wake the dead.

"Is that you, Alice?" I hear him call out. His voice sounds like sandpaper—run ragged by cigarettes and clotted blood. "Come get me, you bitch."

I roll to my side and find some combination of arm and leg positioning that allows me to gather myself to my knees and to standing.

"Yeah, it's me."

"I got your knife, Alice."

"I got your finger," I return. "It's bigger than anything else you've ever put in my mouth."

I brace myself against the wall and lurch into the kitchen on my right leg, where I ricochet from countertop to countertop before I arrive at the couch—his throne.

A dim smile pulls at his cheeks as he raises the knife in his right hand to point it towards me. The gaping wound in his stomach gurgles with his every movement. His body is whole, but his left side seems disconnected somehow, lifeless.

"Come give me a hug," he taunts. A trail of blood drips from the side of his mouth as he speaks. "It's your own life you put into me, Alice, just as I did to you. We're one now."

I stagger forward, and he laughs, the tip of his knife aimed at my chest.

"So come give me a hug. What's wrong with a little self-love?" He smiles again. His teeth are smeared in red tar.

I fall upon him, and I know his blade enters me when our bodies collide, but all I feel is a loss of breath as I descend upon him in a flurry of fists and nails.

I dig my fingers into his eyes, and he cries out as I push past the viscid, jellied resistance. When his body shudders, I pull back to watch as his hand feels blindly for the damage I've done to him.

"Is that all you—" I begin, but I am stopped by my panting. I look down to find the butt of the knife protruding from my chest. A feeling of sick washes over me, and I think I am going to throw up. And suddenly, his screaming is intolerable. It colludes with my nausea and dizziness, and I need it to stop.

I pull at the end of the knife and remove it from my body, surprised by its slice of delicate pain. A cascade of blood pours from the wound. My hands are frenzied and trembling as I hold it. I need him to suffer. But I also need him to stop fucking screaming.

I plunge it back into the gored abyss of his gut, but it only exacerbates his torment. His voice works itself into a high-pitched screech, and I need him to shut the fuck up.

I retake the knife and rip it across his abdomen. His flesh opens like a flaccid mouth, and his organs pour forth like regurgitated meat. Finally, there is silence.

My body deflates on top of his, blood draining from me and mixing into the fluids between us. The gel we make sticks our skin together as it dries. But I don't want to be stuck to him. I don't want to have anything to do with him.

My outrage grows as I sit with the pain swelling within my war-torn body. I shift my eyes to his corpse, and I am overcome by indignation that his vacant vessel rests easily—a body that deserves to be desecrated. But my indignation won't bring him back to life. No amount of anything will bring him back to life, except, perhaps, the book.

KHILLJOY MEMORIAL HOME

MATT HENSHAW

AT KHILLJOY MEMORIAL HOME, our team of well-trained and experienced mortuary scientists will make your funeral one to remember. We specialize in services and preparations that are a cut above the competition. Below is a selection of the options available to the bereaved.

My Corpse Companion: For the mourner who just needs to see their loved one every day and a picture won't do, this package is truly worth more than a thousand words. Marvel at the art that can be wrought by our team of experts as we make a one-of-a-kind manikin out of your loved one. To account for rigor and atrophy, we inject a pliable but sturdy clay to provide for life-like musculature. Bones are fitted with metal beams for additional support. Then we will work with the bereaved to pose the body in whatever jaunty position you choose—for the military man, perhaps a salute; or for the man about the house, reclined with a frosty can of beer in their hand. We can even create a pose that would be impossible for the living to accommodate (joints bending opposite from their 'natural' state). Once the body is positioned, we apply a clear polymer to the epidermis level to limit decay, and then we will install the corpse in your home for years of enjoyment. If, at some point, you want the position to be changed, a nominal $1000 fee for rework will be charged for labor.

Ashes to Ashes to Talisman: We have onsite a state-of-the-art crematorium which can be utilized for this package. Hair and skin remnants are reserved before the rest of the body is sent for burning. The ashes are then collected and pressed into a reproduction of the deceased. Your bespoke talisman is then wrapped in the tanned skin, and hair is affixed accordingly to the head, armpits, and genital region. "My little Bruce fits conveniently in my purse, and I can take him out to dinner, the opera, or my gym! My friends can't believe the craftsmanship! Thank you, Khillljoy!" exclaims one extremely happy widow. Talisman outfits offered for an additional fee.

Funeral Feasts: For customers wanting to share a Last Supper with their dearly departed, our staff will prepare a meal you will not forget. Sous chefs will receive the corpse at our back bay entrance and begin to delicately remove the sweetest of morsels from the cadaver. Liver, kidneys, pancreas, lungs, tongue, sweetbreads, and more will be extracted from the deceased and inspected for quality based on the deceased and survivor's wishes. The body will then be sewn up discretely to hide the harvest. The parts are then taken to our kitchen, where a three-course meal will be prepared. At Khilljoy Memorial Home, we specialize in Latin American, American Southwest, BBQ, Asian, and Mediterranean menus based on available organs and the size of the party. The meal can be served cafeteria style in our banquet room or upon the corpse at our head table. Fluids extracted from the body during the embalming process may be reserved for beverages for an extra fee.

Conjugal Services: Couples who vow "'til death do us part" may be delighted to know that death need not mean the end of intimacy! Using a proprietary process of internal lubrication, ducts, pumps, motors, and wireless speakers, spouses or partners who just can't say goodbye without one last roll in the hay can couple with their corpses in our discreet conjugal cloisters. The corpses are affixed with appropriate hardware reflecting the desires of the living partner, allowing for all manner of intercourse (genital, anal, oral, nasal, and more!). Customers remark at how lifelike the motions created by their thrusting and the motor elements installed in the hip and jaw bones are: "I felt like we were having sex like we did in our youth!" reports one very satisfied mourner. Post-coital disease testing offered for a nominal charge, which is waived if the family consents to filming and recycling of any leavings.

Fireworks and Ordinates Spectacular: Imagine the delight of the mourning party when they see their deceased ignite and explode in a glorious conflagration of fire and viscera! The corpse will be packed with all manner of fireworks and ordinance explosives. On an evening of your choosing, we'll begin the show with the lighting of genital and nipple sparklers, which will serve as fuses for M80s,

Screaming Tops, Black Cats, and other various explosives affixed with epoxy to limbs and digits. But that is only the beginning, the main event consists of a complex array of armaments timed to explode the inner guts of the dead. With this package, we forgo the usual harvesting of organs and fluids for maximum impact. Picture the smiles on your bereaved, sticky faces illuminated by the light of your loved one in the skies above, raining down all manner of entrails. Includes site fee for Koombs Farm location. Safety glasses provided free of charge, tarps for the front row extra.

From The Mouths of Babes: For this package, designed for remains of children under 12, parents will delight at hearing their children "sing" one last hymn of thanks before interment. We are sensitive to the unusual requests that come from parents whose offspring were taken from them "too soon," and we are happy to accommodate. Engineers have perfected a combination of small yet strong remote-controlled fans which direct air out of the lungs, past the larynx, and out of the mouth. An accordion style bellows moves and shapes the mouth to make the various sounds of songs. We can work with any of your child's favorite songs that they would sing in life over and over and over, and recreate a reasonable facsimile of such. Infants and even stillborn or aborted fetuses can be outfitted in a similar fashion to "speak" for their "mama" or "papa." Accompaniment by our staff organist for an extra charge.

Rage Room Service: At Khilljoy Memorial Home, we appreciate that not everyone is sad to see their loved one pass away. Some are happy. Very happy.

But along with that happiness can also come the desire for retribution for wrongs done to them. For those customers seeking closure through catharsis, we are pleased to offer a new outlet for those feelings. At the family's request, we can station the body in our new Rage Room facility a mere 1 mile from our main building, where for 1-, 2- or 4-hour blocks of time, "mourners" armed with bats, sticks, and any items they wish to bring from home (perhaps old dead Dad's hammer) can mercilessly work out their emotions. This popular option has left our customers feeling variously "relieved," "rejuvenated," and "feeling like a large weight has been lifted." You, too, can experience the satisfying thwack and squelch of wood caving in fat and bone, and watching the carcass devolve into a pile of offal, blood, skin, and bone before your very eyes! A cleaning fee will be charged. Khilljoy Memorial Home is not responsible for injuries incurred as a result of enthusiastic activity.

Post-Burial Services: At Khilljoy Memorial Home, we understand that the grief process can make it difficult to come to decisions "in the moment." We are here for you throughout your grieving process. It is not unusual for our customers to come back to us days, weeks, or even months after the body has been buried, requesting whether we can fashion a memorial to their loved one. We enthusiastically respond, "Yes!" Thanks to our unique relationship with local and state governments, we can disinter the carcass from the local graveyard and work with the remains to create a tribute worthy of your devotion. Certain services listed above can be performed given the time passed and remaining biological matter, or we can work with you to create something truly special. One musician customer requested their bride, buried for 9 days, be made into a kind of bagpipe. Fortunately, swamp gasses which had collected in the cadaver caused the body to bloat. We made the blowstick out of a hollowed-out femur bone, with the aperture consisting of her leathery, desiccated vaginal lips. The tenor and bass sticks were then constructed from arm and shin bones. An innovative staff member used her sagging, rotten breasts as bellows, which could be pumped to move air throughout the instrument. Needless to say, the customer was beyond excited to try it out, and the somber tones he generated moved all of our staff to tears. Another musician and luthier worked with our staff to fashion a lute from his friend's skull, intestine, hair, and skin. You can hear him at open mic nights years later still strumming his fantastic instrument. But please don't think we just build instruments, your imagination is our limit.

As you can see, here at Khilljoy Memorial Home, we are committed to providing you and your deceased with the kind of post-life experience that will have you feeling like you can't wait for your own death. We accept major credit cards, cash, and checks, and can work with your budget to create a payment plan if need be. We look forward to serving you and your needs.

Boner

Christine Morgan

IT WAS A bit of a lark, don't you know, just a prank, just a jolly good jape. That's all it was ever meant to be! Nothing like . . . well, like this!

I never did hear who started off the affair. He's kept mum, whoever he is . . . or, was. At first, no doubt, to duck the wrath of the faculty; no sense of humor among that crowd, not a drop. You'd think, at this level of education, one would be above a visit to the Headmaster's office, there to be made to take down one's trousers and bend over the desk and . . . however, I digress.

Later on, I suppose our merry mischief-maker was enjoying the anonymous notoriety of it all, everyone speculating, trying to guess who could be behind such a sly caper. Then other chaps began getting in on the fun. Became something of a thing, didn't it, hey-what? A sporting contest to outdo the others. A challenge, of sorts, to see how long it'd keep up, how long until those dotty old professorial fossils caught on. There'd have been rollicking hell to pay by that point, but with the blame so far-spread among so many, they'd never single out a sole culprit.

As it should be, you know. United we stand, divided we fall. All for one, one for all. In it together, through thick and thin. Nothing for forging life-long bonds as being schoolmates, now, is there?

I mean to say, really, what could they have done? Given every man-jack of us the bare-bottomed over-the-desk treatment? As if the Headmaster could manage the strain! It'd fair to have killed him, I should think. His shriveled ancient organ couldn't have had the stamina of his younger days. My great-uncle was much the same toward the end. It just up and gave out on him one day, and that was all she wrote. Sad, it was. My great-aunt was fair to inconsolable—

What? His heart, of course; what on Earth else?

At any rate, I've digressed again. Terribly sorry. It's the shock of it all, don't you know? Enough to knock a bloke fair off his game. What we witnessed, what we went through—those of us who survived—look me square-on eye to eye and tell me you wouldn't have been shaken like a martini! The aftermath alone should tell enough of the tale. Have you been in there? Have you seen it? Smelled it? Bring a strong man to his knees, it would. Some of the bobbies, first on the scene, took one look and one whiff and fainted dead away.

How could such an unnatural atrocity even be possible? I shudder to wonder. In fact, I refuse to speculate. Well above and beyond me, that stuff. Leave such otherworldly matters to the vicars, I always say. Or those paranormalist what-have-yous, calling up the dearly departed from the Other Side.

As I said, it just started off as a bit of a lark. A bit

of fun. Something to enliven the general tedium and malaise. You try sitting in one of those lecture halls hour after hour, day after day, a hard wooden seat numbing the nethers, the air thick with chalk dust while the likes of Professor Crumberley drones on and on.

Still and all, everyone signed up for his classes, and never mind how the upper-years would try to warn us off. We didn't believe them, thought they were pulling a fast one on the under-years to deprive us of what luscious fruits of learning they'd already enjoyed.

Oh, but no, they'd say. It won't be like you're thinking, not by half. You'll be disappointed. Not to mention bored beyond tears; old Crumby's got a voice like a lowing steer and a cadence like a metronome and he'd put you right to sleep if not for the utter nether-numbing, leg-cramping discomfort. No amount of 'visual learning aids' will make up for it, we're telling you.

Still, hope springeth eternal in the human soul, or some such rot, am I right? Sooner or later, in the studies of Anatomy and Anthropology, why, sooner or later, one would expect, there's bound to be tits! Slides and photographs, don't you know, of those remote tribes, where the native women go about wearing next-to-nothing, and I'm not talking next-to-nothing after the manner of the new bathing costumes all the rage these days . . . not that I'm knocking the new bathing costumes either; I enjoy a peek at a knee or a shoulder as much as the next bloke. Even so, quite a bit different, isn't it, from what you might behold on a jungle expedition, hey-what?

As for Anatomy, well, some of us figured, there'd have to be drawings and diagrams at the very least. Be a chance, wouldn't it, to glean a sense of the actual, you know, design. The downstairs undercarriage, as it were. French postcards and Art Appreciation courses will only carry a fellow so far. Never hurts to have a little something extra to stoke the furnace late in the lonely night and all.

To be sure, eyefuls of willies and wangers are also part of that bargain, as if we don't have an abundance of those already on display around here, what with communal showers and shared dormitory quarters and the like. But, some have a preference for such, and who am I to judge? To each their own, as they say. Not as if we all haven't partaken of our share of experiments. And it's just healthy good fellowship, don't you agree? No one wants to be the Bashful Billy sitting out the occasional—or weekly—circle-jerk, now, do they?

I digress yet again, but you must understand, this is rather quite difficult. Those lads were my schoolmates, my chums! Even the ones who were right bastards I'd just as soon see pushed down a flight of stairs, like Hollings, didn't deserve to be . . . to . . . didn't deserve . . . that.

Where was I? Ah yes, Crumby and his Anatomy lectures. Suffice to say, on the tits-front, it was rather a letdown at best and an off-put at worst. The one picture he showed us of a full female nude, well, it was an autopsy photo. When she's been Y-sliced from collarbones to waist, then laid open, oh, there's tits all right, but they're inside-out displaced mounds of fatty tissue hanging into her armpits, baring her sternum for all the world to see. Nor does it help when an incision's been made round the back of her head from temple to temple, then the scalp peeled forward to lay over her face in a concealing hairy drape of skin. Even if you can, lower down, actually see the, ah, hedge gate to her garden of delights, as it were, the rest of it's a mood-breaker to be sure. The most libidinous of libidos might fail to rise to the occasion under such circs.

So, there, instead, we found ourselves, while Crumby droned through facts we could've just as easily read in the textbooks, him deciding it was best to begin clear back with elementary biology and evolution, that Darwin fellow and all, natural selection and survival of the fittest. Real thing for tortoises and cormorants, he had, Darwin, or so I've heard. If I'm going to sail halfway round the world to exotic distant islands, call me barmy, but I'd prefer the local wildlife to be more, shall we say, mammalian.

At any rate, the lecture hall, and Boner, that's what you want to hear about, isn't it? How it went from a silly nonsense to . . . to what happened.

Blimey. Hits you again, doesn't it? All those chaps dead. Cut down in their prime, as it were. Who's to tell their families, that's what I'd like to know. Or, on second thought, I wouldn't. I'll have my hands full with my own. The mater and pater were against me coming to university here, wanted me closer to home, at the pater's alma mater, so to speak. But Pims and Rogerton were here—we'd been close as quarters back in our knickerbocker days—and what with Battenby and Wilkins also signing on, how could I not? Birds of a feather and all that.

The lecture hall, yes, yes, the lecture hall. We had our desks in strict rows, our hard wooden nether-numbing seats. Busts of academics and philosophers up along the walls, Greeks and whatnot, Aristotle, Plato, that bunch. Straight in front, Crumby's lectern and file cabinets, stacks of books, reams of papers. The projector dead-center, the screen a pull-down jobbie. Behind the desk, a blackboard, you know the sort, in a frame and on wheels. Behind the blackboard, and stretching out to the corners, bookshelves and more cabinets and a jumble sale of taxidermied trophies, ceremonial headdresses, suits of armor, and assorted whatnot.

And Boner.

Supposedly, Boner was there to serve as another visual learning aid. A medical skeleton, the kind they hook together with wires instead of tendons, the foot-bone's connected to the shin-bone, the shin-bone's connected to the thigh-bone, and so on. Only, if you've ever given one of those ossiferous fellows an up-close once-over, it's hardly so simple. Foot-bone? Foot-bone, my foot; must be a dozen or more bones in a single foot alone! For a total of something like, what, two hundred in a body altogether?

At any rate . . . and just as I don't know who did it, I don't know who spotted it first . . . but Crumby was going on about Cro-Magnons or some such rot—though I will tell you, the chapter on Homo Erectus drew its share of jokes too—and we're sitting there counting the minutes until lunch, trying to work some feeling back into our backsides. Then, down in the front right corner, there's a stirring, a perking up. It spreads in a ripple effect of nudges and whispers, subtle pointing, smirks and snickers. Soon, we're all looking round to see what's the distraction—all but old Crumby, droning away occipital this and prognathous that—and what a pip, there's Boner, only someone's repositioned his arm so the tip of one finger is knuckle-deep up a nostril.

I mean to say, how could you not have a chuckle? The lecture hall skeleton mining for the green gold? Not that there'd be any green gold to be found, I'm sure; Boner was dry as unbuttered toast, any mucal moisture of the nasal cavities long since long gone.

Still, it was funny.

That's how it started. That's all it was. Each day, we're waiting for old Crumby to notice, placing bets. Then, a week or so later, we take our seats and, wouldn't you know, instead of the classic finger-up-the-nose gag, there's Boner, two fingers raised, flipping the V!

Well, I say! I nearly fell out of my seat! Had to fake a coughing fit to cover the laughter!

Soon it got so you could hardly wait for Crumby's next lecture, just to see what Boner might have in store. Once, it was a very sharp and snappy proper military salute. Another time, over the span of several days, we had the hands over eye-sockets, ear-holes, and naked-toothed mouth, you know, see no evil speak no evil or however it goes.

It got more intricate as the term went on. Boner, arms akimbo or arms crossed over his empty rib cage. Boner, knees pushed in and hands folded at pelvis, as if either in dire need of a wee or having just taken a cricket pitch bang into the wedding tackle. Boner, caught doing the Highland Fling.

By then, of course, it wasn't the work of a sole perpetrator. Oh, no. Far from. Far, far, far from. Half the class or more were in on it by the time someone upped the ante and began bringing in accessories. Hats and wigs and props from the dramatics department, don't you know? One particularly brilliant bugger dug up a plaster skull used in a production of Hamlet; if I'd found out who that clever cove was, I'd've given him a right hearty clap on the back.

We had Pirate Boner with eyepatch and cutlass. We had Jester Boner with motley fool's cap and bells. We had Boner in blonde braids and Brunhilde breastplate, and Minstrel Show Boner, and Indian Chief Boner, and Explorer Boner in pith helmet holding a toy snake. Once, we came in and there was Boner wearing full mortar-board, robe, and mantle, as if the Headmaster himself decided to put in a guest appearance.

Through it all, old Crumby remained oblivious. I mean to say, how? To be sure, he was half-deaf and half-blind already, stooped nearly double with a beard like tangled cobwebs, but, honestly! One has to wonder how he makes his way from pillow to piss-pot in the night!

Well, that is, one did have to wonder. Not of much import anymore, now, is it? Not with Crumby . . . at least it was quick, isn't that what they say? And he certainly never saw it coming. Bit of a mercy, I suppose. A mercy the rest of us didn't get to share.

Yes, yes, I'm getting there. Have to work up to it, don't you know?

We filed in with our usual anticipation. I do think by that point old Crumby had at least noticed that much, the increased avid interest, no one ever tardy for class. As we took our seats and he shuffled to the lectern, all student eyes—all pupil's pupils? Sorry, yes, dreadful, but I've told you this is difficult for me, and if a chap can't keep a stiff upper lip, is some black-gallows humor too much to allow?

At any rate, there's old Crumby, mumbling over his notes, and the rest of us looking to see what new hijinks might be afoot.

Oh, it was a masterpiece, I'll give you that. A magnum opus, to be sure. Genuine performance art. Someone went to a good deal of trouble rigging the trick. Which, come to think, may be why we were so slow to react . . . thought it was part of the show, didn't we? Until it was too late and the grisly reality set in.

But, there stood Boner, perusing a periodical. Upon initial glimpse, the tableau seemed nothing too elaborate . . . most notable and odd was how a bath-towel—the regular terrycloths we have in the showers—had been not wrapped around his hipbones but strung across in front of him at waist-level, like a curtain. Odd, as I said, but then the attention was inevitably drawn to the periodical itself, clutched in Boner's thin white phalanges.

Which, of course, is where the snickering began; we all recognized, even at a classroom's distance, a catalog of ladies' intimates when we saw one! Fair to say half of us likely had one similar tucked under the mattress in our dormitories. The cover might be discreetly demure, but those inner pages were another story! Curvaceous beauties in corsets and bloomers . . . why, the stocking section alone was well worth the price of admission, hey-what?

Now, this, you see, this took the mischief to a new level. What had been merely impish or inappropriate before had strayed into naughtiness outright . . . but then, with a flawless timing one just has to envy, whoever had orchestrated today's exhibition unleashed the coup-de-grace. At the tug of some unseen trigger, the line holding the terrycloth towel dropped away, and . . .

I shouldn't laugh, I know. Even without taking into account the horrors that followed, it crossed a line, it was crass, it was crude . . . but dashed if it also wasn't bloody ball-busting hilarious!

Boner had a boner!

An animal femur of some sort, obtained from the butcher shop in the village more than likely, or our own school kitchen. Perhaps the remnants of a leg of mutton or roast joint of beef, perhaps a ham-hock; I couldn't say. But, there it was, long as your forearm and as thick around! One end wired into the hollow of his pelvis, the other end . . . sorry . . . the other end protruding . . . no . . . jutting . . . at the jauntiest, proudest, most audacious angle . . .

Do give me a moment. You had to have been there. You had to have seen it in situ. If you had, you'd understand.

To complete the picture, the hand not occupied with the holding of the catalog was indeed otherwise occupied, phalanges curled to the stiff ivory girth in a manner most familiar to every last one of us.

We tried, give us credit for that much at least. We tried, we earnestly did, to hold it together. An entire desperate roomful, red-faced and shaking from our stoic efforts, the occasional stifled snort escaping . . . we tried, but, in the end, well . . .

Pims broke first, and then it was a dam giving way. A tidal wave. Oh, we were laughing, we were whooping and howling and banging on our desks. Some chaps fell from their seats, literally rolling in the aisles.

This, also, old Crumby noticed. Could hardly miss it, could he? Half-blind and half-deaf was no match for such an uproar of sheer pandemonium. A sheaf of notes fell from his startled, palsied grasp. He gawked at us, purely gobsmacked, incredulous. Soon, no doubt, to wax wroth and indignant . . . or, he would have done, if he'd had the chance.

He did not, and on this, I will stake my good name and reputation, see Boner posed in such flagrant shamelessness.

Nor did he see it when . . .

Remember, I've told you, we were so taken in by the cleverness of the scheme, at first, we thought this was part of it too. Marionette strings or mechanical armatures or the like, the way they have those cunning little figures in German clocks.

We very quickly realized, however . . .

I say, must we really go into the gory details? Doesn't the crime scene speak for itself?

All right, then, all right. Come this far, haven't I? In for a penny and whatnot. Send me off to the nuthatch, but I know what I saw.

Boner moved.

Of his own accord and volition. Flung the catalog—it flapped through the air like a butterfly with wings patterned in corseted bosoms and stockinged legs—and sprang from the stand upon which he'd patiently endured so much abuse.

The how of it, him lacking muscle and tendon and all, I'll not hazard a theory. Nor will I speculate as to the function of his senses . . . bereft of eyes but for hollow sockets, bereft of ears, bereft of anything beyond bone and wire, he saw and he heard and he moved and he knew.

And he moved. With a rattling clatter, audible through the cacophony of mirth about to become a cacophony of terror, he moved.

Old Crumby never saw it coming, I repeat and maintain and will swear to that. He'd only just begun to open his mouth to berate our unruliness when Boner leapt, monkeylike, spiderlike, onto his stooped back. And . . . well . . . and . . .

The boner with which Boner had been indecorously equipped? Old Crumby got it right in the occipital.

Crack! went the skull, like a brittle china cup, and out from Crumby's still-opening mouth spewed not stern words of professorial discipline but an absolute geyser of blood and chunky lumps I suppose must've been his educated brains. These were followed in very short order by a set of dentures and some shattered teeth as the knobby business end of the femur affixed to Boner's pelvis burst on through.

Crumby was dead in an instant, I'd swear to that too. He and his lectern went over in a tremendous crash. By then, in a withdrawal as violent as the means of entry, Boner had extricated his bony battering ram from the ruins of Crumby's breached cranial bastion and turned toward the rest of us. With, I dare say, what could only be described as murderous intent.

BONER

The cacophony and pandemonium had not ceased; no, far from! It had, however, undergone seamless transition from laughter to screams. My own among them, I don't mind telling you. Bravery and courage are all fine and well in their place, but we had gone well off the rails into uncharted territory by then.

As for particular details of the next several moments, it's hard to be precise. There was, understandably enough, utter chaos. Erupting from our seats, desks toppling and books flying every which-way . . . pushing and shoving and stumbling over each other . . . years of ingrained unity, rah-rah school spirit and bonhomie, chucked aside . . . beans to that all for one, one for all business; it was every man for himself and devil take the hindmost!

I remember seeing Pims, my lifelong chum, who'd been the one to laugh first, the crack in the dam unleashing the torrent, spun sideways in a crimson spray by a swipe of Boner's raking phalanges, throat slashed into shreds and furrows. I remember seeing Hollings, that right bastard, knock down and trample another chum, Wilkins, bolting for the door. I remember someone—couldn't see whom—drop to his knees in a posture of pleading surrender, only to have Boner's bony boner rammed into his face with the force, and effect, of a sledgehammer to a watermelon.

I also remember Wilderidge, the school middleweight bare-knuckles boxing champion, stripping off his blazer to confront Boner in shirtsleeves, fists raised. His form was excellent. So was his footwork. Bob and weave, duck and dodge, pistoning a flurry of economical blows, none failing to meet their mark.

The trouble with that, though, you see, the trouble with that was . . . well . . . for one thing, throwing punches at a skeleton, frankly, isn't much use, now, is it? Nothing but bone to hit, is there? Can't very well wind him with a hard compact jab to the breadbasket when there's no breadbasket, nor lungs to hold wind, for that matter. And what good is a dead-cert prizewinning uppercut to the ole knockout button to ring a foe's bell and put him down for the count when all he's got is bare jawbone and empty skull?

For another, not as if Boner felt bound by the accepted rules and etiquette of gentlemanly fisticuffs or fair play. Hardly sporting, that.

Still and all, can't fault Wilderidge for trying, even if all he accomplished was to scrape his own skin bloody in the process of rocking Boner's head back once or twice and maybe cracking a rib. He stood his ground, you've got to give him that. Which is certainly more than the rest of us did.

Cost him dearly too . . . when Boner went for a shot to the breadbasket in return, suffice to say, it connected. It more than connected. Wilderidge's shirtfront, and indeed torso . . .

The tricky bit about guts, don't you know, is, when you see them in the anatomical drawings or cutaway models, it's all nice and orderly, a place for everything and everything in its place. Neatly labeled too, more often than not. You can, at a glance, tell a liver from a gallbladder and a stomach from a spleen. When you see them, instead, yanked out in a large purplish sloppy-wet mess to splat unceremoniously onto the lecture hall floor . . .

Suffice also to say, it put me off steak-and-kidney

pie for the rest of my life; can't speak for anyone else, but I suspect I'm hardly alone in the sentiment.

Meanwhile, during Wilderidge's last stand, there'd come quite a logjam in the corner by the exit. Door opens inward, don't you know, but in their haste to escape, half the class had gotten packed up against it in a crush of struggling bodies and no one with the presence of mind to make room. They were fish in a barrel, and Boner, shaking loose clots of viscera like a dog shedding water, waded right on in.

Others had fled to the storage closet or taken refuge behind cabinets or overturned desks. A more enterprising few went for the windows, and when Battenby seized my arm, shouting we had to make ourselves scarce, such appeared to my reasoning to be the best option. Of our other childhood chum, Rogerton, I'd completely lost track, but there was no time to waste.

The windows in the room being rather inconveniently high, we were called upon to demonstrate some solidarity after all, piling furniture enough to let the more agile lads scramble up, swing wide the panes, and assist their fellows. I spared one final glance at the exit-door corner, which had become such a tangled mass of limbs both flailing and inert I could scarcely determine where one body left off and another began. The only recognizable figure was Boner, knee-deep in their midst, needing only a cloak and a scythe to be the very Grim Reaper incarnate, wreaking bloody slaughter.

Battenby and I climbed together, hup-hup tally-ho, diving headlong through the window and barely heeding the ten-foot plunge to the greensward below.

He fractured a wrist, and I turned an ankle, but we did not let that stop us for a hot second as we raced for safety.

So, there it is, there you have it, whether you believe me or not. Oh, I've heard the talk going round. I know your theories, your suspicions. Like to blame it all off on some of us, wouldn't you? Student madness, must be! That's what you're telling yourselves, isn't it?

After all, the only skeleton you've turned up in the carnage could only be nothing more than a harmless visual learning aid thrown askew from its stand during such a ruckus. Just another piece of forensic evidence to be labeled and logged and forgotten about. Not anything playing possum, as it were. Not anything deadly dangerous that should bloody well be destroyed before it's too late!

I see those looks. Think I've gone full bananas, don't you?

Well, you just ask the others, the chaps who survived. Ask Battenby. Ask Argyle; I saw him down the hall. Ask any of us.

We all saw it. We'll all tell you the same.

It was Boner. And, mark my words, Boner's not done with us yet.

FETID

SUSAN SNYDER

HE FIRST THING I noticed when I regained consciousness was the water. I was sitting in about a foot of it, propped up against a cold, rough wall. My eyes were blurry, but I tried to get a grasp on my surroundings. A very dim light came from above. As I strained my neck to look up, my muscles screamed. There was a square opening about eight feet in diameter and what seemed like a mile away.

What is this?

Panic struck me like a surge of electricity to my gut. Despite the pain, I whipped my head side to side, desperate to recognize anything that would explain this situation. The water sloshed around me in my efforts and splashed my face. I settled down my movements, and my tongue reached out to taste the droplets. It was fresh water, not salty. There was staleness to it, like a drinking cup left too long on the kitchen counter. An unpleasant aftertaste lingered in the back of my throat. This water was fresh, yes, but not clean.

What is this?

My mind searched memories at a frantic pace for a hint of what got me here. Every cell began to dance with anxious energy. A panic attack was starting. I knew that all too well.

"No. No. No. No."

My hands slapped the water in time with my words. Then my right hand hit my thigh, submerged just under the water's surface. It didn't find firm flesh but a gaping tear of jagged tissue. I felt no pain, just surprise. As I let my hand explore the wound, I felt the hardness of bone under a thin sheet of viscera. I turned my sore neck to the left and vomited. Then, blackness took over.

The light was brighter when my eyes reopened. It was midday now. Before, it must have been early in the morning. Now I could see more of the space I was in, but the corners were still filled with shadows.

The cistern was old. The interior was made of brick, with a layer of concrete on the exterior. I knew this because I had seen these before. They lay among remnants of dead and scorched trees within Bastrop State Park. The massive fire of 2011 had all but decimated the Lost Pines Forest. Now, it was slowly regenerating. Hints of its former life still remained here, though. Ranger stations that used to pepper the park needed to collect rainwater for their toilets and sinks. The cabins were gone, but the cisterns remained.

I had spent a lot of time in this charred forest. Mostly, I went off the grid into the closed area north of Park Road. The Park Service was monitoring resource recovery here, and the area was closed to the public. For me, it held more than the skeletons of pine trees. Despite the slim chance of being caught by a ranger, I couldn't resist it.

When I was really young, my father and I visited Mount St. Helens, which had erupted in 1980 in the Cascades of the Pacific Northwest. It was the twentieth anniversary of the disaster, but dead trees still lined the hills like toothpicks. They were all facing outward from the volcano, plastered down by the force of the blast. In some spots, the land still resembled the surface of the moon. Yet, within this devastation, the forest was returning. Small flowers were budding from the ground, and animals were growing in number. Hope had sprung from a disaster of almost biblical proportion.

The Lost Pines reminded me of that. It was my St. Helens, but close to home. Every weekend, I wandered off the paths into the north part of the park. Life was returning here too. Over the months, deer could be seen through the scarred and blackened trees that presided like sentinels over the landscape. Pockets of grass and bushes, and sometimes even wildflowers, popped up in bursts of color from the grey earth.

What really drew me here was that no one was ever around. Especially my uncle. Well, not in the way he was before.

Throbbing pain from my injury was consuming me. I gingerly bent my right leg to bring my thigh out of the shallow water and into the light.

"Oh my god," I whispered to no one. My voice sounded hollow in the confined space.

The wound began right below my groin and wrapped halfway around the side of the leg. It ended just above the knee. Torn edges of skin were bubbled with red tissue and, in places, white gelatinous blobs of fat. The position of the leg, with the knee bent and my foot on the ground, opened the wound. I saw inside to the meat of muscle and the white tendrils of connective tissue that covers the bone. There was no blood. The water had washed it away. The healthier skin of my thigh, knee, and lower leg were streaked with pink scratches. My mind couldn't bring up a plausible explanation for this. The pain wouldn't let my brain function properly. One thought I could muster was an incredulous one. I wanted to smother it instantly, but it circled around me like a shark. This looked like the bite of a large animal.

Looking around the cistern, I tried to ignore the sting of my thigh and focus on what was happening to me. The space was about eight feet by eight feet, made with bricks whose mortar was starting to crumble from age and moisture. Shallow water sat at the bottom. It wasn't cold. The water temperature barely registered on my skin. It was summer in central Texas, so the air was cooler inside the cistern than it would be outside. It smelled stuffy, and the atmosphere was rife with humidity. The opening at the top allowed daylight in but looked to be partially covered by the trunk of a fallen tree. My best guess was that the entrance was twenty feet away. No ladder led to the top. There was nothing to climb to get me the hell out of there. Even if there was, my leg might prevent it.

I had to try to stand, to walk around the space, to explore any possible way out. My right leg was already bent, so I braced myself on the brick wall behind me. Bending my left leg, I pushed up on both feet to a standing position. For just one sweet instant, I felt nothing. Then my right leg buckled underneath me, and I fell to the floor with a splash, hitting my tailbone on the concrete. All my wind was knocked out of me, and I gasped for breath. Finally, I sucked in a gulp of air, only to quickly let it back out with a scream of agony.

"Fuuuuck!"

Tears came as I continued to alternate between screams and profanity. I was aware that this behavior was not helping me in any way, but it was all I could do at the moment. I stopped in the middle of a scream when I noticed another sound in my space. At first, I thought it could be an echo, a false mimic within the walls of the cistern.

"Hello?"

Louder.

"HELLO?"

There was no echo. So I screamed at a volume and octave I didn't even think I was capable of. Again, no echo answered me. Rather, the response came from the top of the cistern.

A deep and guttural sound bellowed from a shadowy figure at the opening. It seemed to match my intensity and desperation. Some of the being's form was behind the fallen trunk, so I couldn't see enough silhouette to make it out. The opening was too far away to recognize what it was, but I was grateful for the distance. This was not human in shape or sound.

Frozen still and silent, I covered my mouth with my wet hands and held my breath. The creature's breathing was rapid and shallow, almost a wheeze. Even twenty feet away, I could hear it clearly in my small chamber. I wondered how long it had been there, looking down at me. My tantrum had kept me distracted enough not to notice. Tears began to roll down my cheeks and pool in my hands, still cupped over my mouth, and I could taste the salt of them.

The figure left the opening amid crackling soil and snapping twigs. I lowered my hands from my face and placed them on my chest. My heartbeat was in palpitations, and I was beginning to hyperventilate. I closed my eyes and rested my head back onto the wall. Drawing in deep breaths through my nose, I let them slowly out through my mouth. This went on for some time, until I felt something tickle the nape of my neck.

It's funny how you can go without noticing something for a while, but as soon as you notice, it's everywhere. I didn't see the spiders at all until I reached for the back of my neck and felt something crawling in my hair. Instinctively, I pulled my hand back, but the spider had already crawled onto it. It was a Daddy

Long Legs, and a big one. I yelped and shook it off, hearing it drop into the water with a soft plop. These were not capable of hurting me and I knew that. My crippling fear of spiders, however, would not allow that sort of rational thought.

There was still enough light to see the walls to the front and sides. My eyes scoured the bricks for signs of any more spiders. I could only spot one on the wall to my right, and it was walking toward me. It was getting close, too close for my comfort. Its body was the size of a pencil eraser, but those legs made the size swell up to that of a quarter.

"Go away," I said softly.

Hearing my words, the spider stopped in its tracks. She looked at me and I looked at her. The fact that I shared my space with spiders made my mouth dry. I felt itchy and paranoid. People called it "the willies." I stared at that spider until the clouds far above faded the daylight enough that I couldn't see her anymore. She didn't make a move. She just stared back. Now, it was too dark to see her or any other bug that lurked in the cistern. A midday summer thunderstorm was coming. The rumbles in the distance confirmed that. At least I hoped the sounds were coming from the storm.

However, that fearful distraction caused me to forget the pain in my leg for a little while. I felt a twinge of gratitude.

The storm never materialized into any rain, which is not uncommon for the area. It probably just sideswiped the park. Eventually, the rumbling faded into a whisper. Without the diversion, the torment of my wound came back with a vengeance, but it cleared the fog from my mind.

I had a fanny pack with me when I went hiking.

It was still a little too dark to see if the pack made it down into the cistern with me. I felt around the water, but my hands found nothing but the concrete floor lined with dirt and bits of debris.

"You're down here somewhere."

Clinging to this possibility, I recalled what I had put in the pack before I left the house. Flashlight, bottle of water, gum, lip balm, cell phone, two-pack of ibuprofen, protein bar, and a ball of tin foil. That ibuprofen would be a godsend. Plus, I needed that ball of foil. I couldn't lose that. As soon as there was enough light to see again, I would find that pack.

I awoke in the middle of the night, or at least I guessed it was the middle of the night. I never wore a watch, always depending on my smartphone to tell time. It was very dark, and the air was damp and thick. My legs had straightened out and were both submerged under the water. Immediately, I bent my legs, trying to keep the wound as dry as I could. The sudden movement of the tender tissue caused me to cry out in anguish.

From the opening at the surface, I got a response. The creature was still there, and it was keeping vigil over me.

My uncle often stared at me as I slept. He didn't know that I knew. I cracked open my eyes just enough to see his reflected shape in my wall mirror, dimly lit by my nightlight. He sat behind my back at the corner of my bed. He did this almost every night. My young mind couldn't piece together why. Not yet. At that time, I felt like he was watching over me, protecting me. That was supposed to be his job now.

An ear-piercing screech hit me like a sledgehammer and set off an instant panic. Ignoring the pain in my body, I sprang into immediate action like I had been shot with electricity. Frantic, I crawled around the space and grasped at every inch of that water. The flesh of my knees scraped raw on the concrete as I dragged my legs. The mounds of skin under my thumbs took the brunt of my weight as I shifted from one hand to the other. One searched for the fanny pack as the other pressed into the tiny pebbles and dirt on the floor. As I reached one darkened corner, I felt soft things fall onto my head, into my hair. The commotion of my movements had woken the spiders. I instinctively shook my head like a dog and continued scouring that space with the desperation of a wild animal caught in a trap. Another howl came from above, and I answered with my own from within.

My left hand touched something that felt like fabric.

121

"Got it."

Instead of feeling relieved, I quickly retreated to the spot where I had initially been sitting, churning the water around me. It was some sort of instinctual act, to go home, to get to safety. Once back at my little piece of the cistern wall, I allowed myself a moment to hold the fanny pack to my chest like a teddy bear. As the thing at the top of the well offered one last bellow, I squeezed it tighter as if to protect it from the noise. My eyes squeezed just as tight until the sound subsided. Again, the creature left the opening. I could hear the movements through the dry brush.

I could focus on the pack now. I hoped that little foil package was still there.

The cell phone was dead from the water. That was expected. There would be no way to tell the time other than the little bit of sky I could see at the top of the cistern. The corner of the fanny pack was torn, almost shredded. That gave me pause and gave more credence to the animal attack theory. I pushed that thought out of my mind and kept on with the task at hand. The lip balm must have fallen out of the hole. The gum and protein bar were waterlogged, but I didn't dare discard them. My heart soared when the flashlight switched on. Immediately, I sent its beam into the seams and lining of the pack, looking for that ibuprofen. There it was, a pack of two. The plastic pouch containing the pills was intact. More importantly, the foil was there. I felt like I won the lottery.

The feeling was short lived as I remembered the water bottle. It was gone. It could still be here, I hoped. My wound was on fire from the activity, and I knew I couldn't take another excruciating journey around the cistern. Not until I rested a bit. My mouth and throat were parched from the screaming and the lack of water. The irony of the situation hit me hard.

Water, water everywhere and not a drop to drink.

I tried to swallow the pills dry. My burning throat was too inflamed to get them down, and I almost lost them when I spat them out into my hands. My injury became furious and began to sear with pain, forcing my attention. Looking down at my thigh, the wound was a crooked smile, toothless and gums bleeding. A large chunk of red muscle seemed to be a wet and ragged tongue.

The first time my uncle violated me, I wasn't sure what was happening. During one of his nightly bouts of staring, he decided to go a bit further. Through the cracks in my eyelids, I watched him through my mirror lean down toward my left ear. His tongue darted out and flicked my earlobe. It was quick, and if I hadn't been watching it, I would have never felt it. I became nauseous, but I couldn't move. I wouldn't let him know that I knew. I felt that somehow gave me some control over him, holding a forbidden knowledge. Besides, who would I tell? My parents were dead, I had no siblings. I was fifteen, yet my uncle held me out of school. He kept me locked in the house and away from prying neighbors. I knew this whole situation was wrong. It was not the way life was supposed to be. Yet, he fed me, let me watch TV, and never hurt me. That night with the tongue was only the start of it.

With the flashlight, I examined the water surrounding me. It looked gray, but that was just due to the concrete floor of the cistern. I scooped a little water up with my free hand and brought it to my nose. It smelled a bit rancid. I just wanted to get those ibuprofen down so badly. They were lodged in the lining of my cheek and tasted bitter. My leg demanded them. By this time, my head was joining the pain party as well. *I might have a concussion*, I thought. *Perhaps I could just chew the pills*, but I knew I would gag, risking reflexively spitting them out. I brought my hand down and brought up a bigger scoop of water. Quickly, I flicked the pills free with my tongue, sipped the water from my palm, and swallowed. I almost gagged anyway. The water was spoiled and warm.

The worst part wasn't the taste of the liquid. It was the chewy bits left behind like some meat you find between your teeth long after a meal. They were tasteless, but the texture was rubbery and off-putting. There was a lot of debris floating around, washed in from rain. Bits of my vomit floated about the surface. There had to be blood and tissue from my leg in the mix. In the back of my mind, I hoped that I hadn't just eaten a spider. More disturbingly, I found the tiny amount of wetness in my mouth and throat just made my thirst into another agony for me to deal with.

The flashlight provided some comfort. I could see into the corners of the space, so at least I was reassured the creature wasn't sitting there, in shadow, watching. There were piles of debris in the corners. Over time, the leaves and twigs had washed in and stacked up. In the beam of light, the leaves of the pile seemed to rustle slightly. I was certain that stuff contained some impressive spiders' nests. Maybe the sudden introduction of a new light source aggravated them. I pushed the thought away. Turning the light toward my leg, I examined the wound closely. My leg was kept bent, and the majority of the injury was drying out. The edges were a deep brown color, but the meat inside still looked fresh and moist. If I moved that leg now, after it had been immobile for a while, it would be extremely painful. That water bottle must be in here somewhere, though. I needed to soothe my thirst and soon. The thought of clean, fresh water was becoming an obsession.

It wasn't an emergency yet, but I knew that I would die of thirst long before I died of hunger. How long was I in here so far? About 24 hours? Surely, I'd figure this all out before it got too desperate. I had some food, albeit soaked with foul water. The food might mask the taste while providing a little moisture. I stuck the flashlight under my chin to free my hands and sent the beam toward the fanny pack. The strap to the pack was shredded, but I was able to tie the two loose ends into a knot. I looped it around my neck so I could keep my hands free and also keep the pack out of the water. Gingerly, I opened the protein bar's packaging. It had a rotten and dank odor. Was the water that bad?

Suddenly, it dawned on me to check the package of foil. It had wedged into the farthest right end of the pack. I had wrapped it pretty tightly, compressing the contents. It amazed me that something that caused me so much pain, that loomed so large in my life, could be turned into something so small and frail. Perhaps this was the cause of the awful smell permeating the protein bar? After all, foil wasn't exactly waterproof, and it had been sitting in the water for almost a whole day.

I carefully began to peel off the foil just enough to see it, to know it was okay. Once assured, I wrapped it back up carefully and stuffed it into the pack. Despite the smell, I ate the bar in two quick bites. As I chewed, the moisture squeezed out and coated my tongue with a mixture of peanut butter and something slightly sour. Forgetting the flashlight was still under my chin, the movement of my jaw caused it to almost drop into the water. I caught it just in time. The beam of light landed on something floating in the water to my immediate right. I grabbed the thing and examined it. There was no mistaking what it was. It was the water bottle, but it had been chewed up like a dog's toy. The liquid was gone.

"Jesus."

I began to weep but held it together so that I didn't cry out what little rancid fluid I had previously ingested. A bit of snot ran down from my nostril to my lower lip and I wiped it away.

My uncle made me cook dinner every night. Usually, he demanded the standard meat and potatoes fare. He had high cholesterol, but an idiot like that never has the forward thinking to take care of himself. He was a man who got what he craved. I was clear evidence of that. His nightly visits had become various shades of rape. His lust for food, however, was ultimately his downfall. He never noticed the missing knife. It was a nice one too. A Mercer German steel chef's knife which I kept very sharp.

He locked me away in my bedroom promptly at 8 p.m., as was protocol. Later, he would use his key to let himself in, no longer attempting to sneak inside. The element of surprise had long faded away. Now he reveled in my fear and anticipation. Yet, I had a hell of a surprise waiting for him that night.

For days prior, I turned over and examined every move I would or could make when he visited me that night. I swished the plan around in my head like a rubber ball in a washing machine. In the hour between the time I was sequestered in my room until the time he came, I fretted so much about it that I began to have one of my panic attacks. This was not a good thing. Those attacks clouded my thoughts and weakened my muscles. They felt similar to having a stroke, at least that's what I always guessed. I had to be ready for this. I began to take very long breaths. I pulled the knife from under my pillow and examined every bit of it, speaking softly to myself as I did.

"Black handle. Blade about six inches long. Word

'Mercer' on the blade. Blade feels colder than the handle. The edges feel sharp."

Finding an object to focus on helped to calm me down. Breathing slower, my mind refocused. Just in time. I heard the key in the lock.

I shoved the knife back under my pillow but kept my hand on the handle. There was no point in pretending to sleep as I did when I was younger. Everything was pretty damn inevitable now. He approached me with his sly cat grin, unzipping his trousers. I allowed him to get on top of me. He shoved my nightgown up around my neck. He lowered his head to my breast and sucked at my nipple aggressively. One hand braced himself on the mattress while the other slid down my belly toward my crotch.

I took a deep breath like I always did before his fingers entered me. This time, it was a wind-up breath. I quickly slid the knife from under my head and sliced at the side of his neck. My uncle whipped his head up instinctively, his mouth leaving my nipple wet and sore. I stabbed him in his left eye. I was careful to bring the blade back out. I couldn't risk it getting stuck in his flesh or eye socket. His blood was beginning to flow over my exposed skin, his writhing and gyrations smearing it into my pores. I felt a combination of strange pleasure and relief.

I brought my knee up to his balls as hard as I could. He rolled off my body enough for me to slip out from under him, lubricated by the blood. He lay on his back and cupped his balls. I stabbed frantically at his hands until he released them. He grabbed at the knife and almost wrenched it from my hands. I jumped off the bed to get out of his reach. In an instant, I was at his side of the bed. He waved his hands in front of his face, trying to ward off the blows. So I took the opportunity to stab his genitals as hard as I could. My uncle managed to connect a hard blow to my cheek, but I was in a frenzy. My screams grew louder and morphed into laughter. I brought the knife up again and slammed it into his other eye. Blinded, he flailed his arms, searching for me. He was still laying on his back, probably too shocked and stupid to try to get away.

I walked up toward the headboard. I positioned myself behind his head, grabbed a fistful of hair, and reared his dumb skull back. I slit his exposed throat but couldn't get the blade to slice through all the way from ear to ear. He kept reaching back with his bloodied hands. I kept swatting at them with the knife.

I plunged the knife into the same wound I had caused before in the side of his neck. The knife sank in deeper this time. I let his head drop back to the pillow. He grunted. Using both hands on the handle, I pulled the blade through his throat to the other side. At this point, his hands had dropped to his sides. He seemed paralyzed with shock and pain. I howled. I sawed at this throat until the knife struck hard bone. Stepping back, I observed my work.

As my uncle gurgled his last gory breath, I tilted his head toward the mirror on my wall. He had no eyes to see his reflection, but I could. I leaned down and gently licked his ear.

In my house, where no one remembered I existed, I spent several days dismembering my uncle. I was too weak to move his body whole. I broke into the garage and used his power saw on his joints. The head was the easiest part to remove. I had already done a lot of the work with the knife. I carefully put each section of his corpse into trash bags. I saw that done on TV in those crime reenactment shows. I found the keys to my uncle's red Dodge pickup and loaded him up in the back. I took a long hot shower and watched the blood and tissue circle the drain and disappear.

I wasn't a very practiced driver, but in that sleepy Texas town, no one was prone to even notice. I imagined a passerby would assume it was my uncle, half-drunk, swerving down Main Street. I wasn't really sure where I was going to dump that awful man, but I saw a sign for Bastrop State Park and I followed it. This was a week before the fire of 2011 and the woods were verdant and lush. I drove deep into the park to the area north of Park Road. There were "No Unauthorized Use" signs here and there, but I paid them no mind. I was pretty sure it was a Tuesday, and by the time I drove my way to that part of the park, it was just about twilight. Not a soul was around.

I was sixteen and not exactly schooled in the ways of body disposal. I took each trash bag, one by one, and tossed them into a ravine about 100 yards off the access road. There was a little creek at the bottom, and each bag hit it with a thick and heavy splash. Someone might find them, but I couldn't think about that now. I was free. I threw my head back and howled with glee and a strength I hadn't felt in my whole life. On the drive home, my thoughts kept returning to the image of the red blood circling the drain and disappearing.

The massive wildfire had burned away the filth of the remains of my uncle. I began to visit the area north of Park Road as often as life allowed me. The slow recovery and regrowth of the park mirrored my own. I had remained close by, moving to Austin from my small town. With a new name, I checked into a women's shelter with a complex story of abuse and abandonment. I told a version of the truth, leaving out a few incriminating details. Over time, my life began anew and I had a job, an apartment, and fewer and fewer nightmares.

Yet here I sat, at the bottom of a cistern, wounded, stalked, and pretty much fucked.

It was morning, and soft light began to illuminate the space once more. I managed to keep my legs bent, and a dry tightness permeated my wound. It stung. My mouth was even drier. I scooped a bit of water to my mouth and sipped just enough to wet my palate. It tasted coppery and foul, and I could imagine all the little organisms and bits of myself swimming around in it.

I unzipped the pack hanging around my neck and removed the foil package. Small and light, the foil's crumpled texture and sharp creases hurt my waterlogged fingertips. Ignoring this, I began to carefully unwrap the foil.

I kept this little treasure with me at all times. It was a souvenir of my power, my ability to overcome anything. At first, I kept the thing in the freezer at the women's shelter, wrapped in cloth and stuffed into a Ziploc baggie. The folks there had a great habit of minding their own business, so I didn't think anyone had ever found it. Even if they did, they would have no clue what they were looking at. A man's penis is unrecognizable once you remove it from the man.

Once I had my own place, I often took it out and examined it. One night, I fell asleep at the kitchen table, the thing by my head. I awoke to a horrible odor, and the penis had started to thaw and decompose. I couldn't put it back in the freezer with my frozen peas and pizza rolls. Wrapped in layers of paper towels, I stuck it in the oven for safekeeping. I never used the damn oven anyway. It kept it dry, and I couldn't smell it much anymore. When I visited the park, I always gingerly wrapped it in foil and carried it in my pack. It seemed only fitting to bring it with me like a talisman, a warning to anyone who dared to fuck with me. I felt empowered with it near me.

As I gazed at the mummified little mound of leathery flesh in the foil wrap, I heard a sound coming from the shadowy corner of the well. A grunt and a quiet splash, as if something shifted its weight.

Jesus, had something gotten in here while I slept?

I felt around for the flashlight but couldn't find it. I must have let it drift away from me in the night. The morning sun was slowly rising, and light was very gradually swelling into the farther reaches of the space. I could just make out the pile of debris in the corner from where I heard the sounds. The leaves and twigs wove together in such a tapestry that it almost seemed like fabric or fur.

It was just a pile of leaves and twigs and that was all. Maybe some spiders' nests. I had imagined the sounds. I had bigger fish to fry at the moment. I needed that flashlight, the comfort of it, the heft of it in my hand. I rewrapped the foil package and stuck it in the fanny pack tied around my neck. Bringing both hands to the concrete floor under the water, I started to stand up. My left leg's strength supported my wounded right leg enough to get me almost all the way up. I braced myself against the wall with my hands as I rose.

Then I froze with both legs slightly bent and my butt propped against the wall. The pile of debris in the corner, now better lit with the rising sun, was standing up as well. I gasped. The debris grew taller. My thighs began to burn with the exertion of holding myself up. I felt water and a more viscous fluid drip out from my damaged thigh and run down my shin. The mass in the corner drew in a long breath and shrieked. I slid down the wall and landed with a thud. I didn't scream. I was not capable of any sound. My wound tore open and screamed for me. My face contorted into a grimace of pain, but my eyes kept fixed on the creature in the corner.

Something bumped up against my ankle, and I twitched in surprise. It was the flashlight. Moving slowly, my fingers found it and brought it up to my chest. I hesitated for a moment. I wondered if I wanted to see this creature in the full exposure of the flashlight's beam. As if reading my thoughts, the monster bellowed again, prompting me into action. I clicked the flashlight on.

Before the light found its face, the shaky beam

afforded me glimpses of the thing's body. Some of the leaves and twigs had fallen away, but some had stayed fast, stuck to some sort of sticky secretion. The visible areas looked glossy with the stuff. The skin of its torso wasn't skin but almost a carapace. The four arms I could see above the water were studded with boils and pustules. They pulsated, or maybe that was just the tremble of the hand holding the flashlight. Finally, I settled the light upon its face.

I saw my uncle. I saw his eyes. There was no doubt that they were his eyes. He began to draw back the corners of his mouth in that godforsaken Cheshire cat grin, the same one he flashed at me when he visited me at night. This time, the grin grew impossibly wide. The creases of the corners of his mouth split open and pincers emerged from either side.

It cocked its head to one side and raised one arm. It pointed at me, at my chest. Perhaps the light was hurting it? Good. Fuck it. Before I could react, the thing was right in front of me. It had moved so rapidly, I could barely discern the movement. It smacked the flashlight from my hand with one of its lower arms and leaned down. The pincers were inches from me and trembling like tuning forks. An arm rose up and pointed again. This time it was close enough to find its target. The slimy claw at the end of the arm was pressing into the pack dangling at the middle of my chest. The eyes of my uncle bore into me with insistence. I knew then what it wanted. There was a flapping noise, and I glanced toward the area between the beast's legs.

There was an orifice right at my eye level, opening and closing. It looked like the mouth of a hungry baby bird. My gaze went back up to its face, to his face. The pincers vibrated more intensely. The flapping grew more aggressive.

Not wanting to make a sudden move, I willed myself into slow motion. The pack was still unzipped. One hand held the pack still while the other retrieved the foil package. I held it out for him to take. He grunted so forcefully that my hair was blown back.

"Okay, okay. I'm sorry." My voice was small and frail, like a little girl.

Without breaking eye contact, I unwrapped my prize and held the small, decimated mound out in my hand. My uncle glanced down at it and back up at me. He took the penis very gently into his pincers and spun around. In an instant, he scaled the brick-and-mortar wall of the cistern and scurried out. I heard the fading sounds of movement as he got further away from the entrance to the cistern. When I was confident he was far enough away, I allowed myself to weep.

I sat for a long time and stared at the wound on my thigh. When I came to the park that day, or yesterday, or whenever that was, that pack was around my waist. The more I thought about it, the more I knew that it was my uncle who attacked my leg. He wanted it, and he knew I had it. He did this to me. He put me here. But he had just missed the target.

I wondered why he hadn't attacked me since then. I was convinced, however, that he would return. Perhaps he would consume me? With my leg in its current condition, there was no escape. I felt a pang of envy as I remembered the ease at which he scrambled up that wall and into the big bright world.

The mangled water bottle floated over to me again. I grabbed and examined it, turning it over in my hands. The torn edges of the plastic were jagged and strong. Perhaps this could be a weapon against him when he returned.

Then it hit me. A cold fear trickled down my spine. I gave it to him. He was whole now. He may have been in a different state, but he was still my uncle. He was still that sexual predator, that deviant piece of shit. He was keeping me here to rape me. He would get his revenge in the most horrific way possible. My mind flashed images of his pincers slicing off my nipples, his clawed arm working its way inside me.

I felt another panic attack coming on strong. My heart raced. I began to sweat. Breathing became shallow and rapid. I pressed the back of my head against the cold brick wall and looked up at the square of visible sky above me, stretching the flesh of my throat. Instead of sky, I saw the monstrous form of my uncle, pincers twitching. There was an addition to his silhouette. I could see something protruding from the orifice between his legs. It wagged like the tongue of a dog.

I pierced the flesh of my neck just below my left ear with the jagged bottle and sawed through as deep as my strength would allow. Blood cascaded over my cool skin. I used the corner of the bottle to spear each of my eyes. He might still use my body to do unspeakable things, but it would only be an empty shell. I didn't feel any pain. Just the warmth of my blood and the sharpness of the fear of what would happen if I remained alive.

Before I lost consciousness, I heard an ear-piercing scream. I managed to choke out a muffled response.

"Fuck you."

Hopefully, my life would circle the drain before he got started.

About the Authors

P.J. Blakey-Novis is a British writer living on the south coast of England. He is the author of six collections of short stories and a horror novella, and has appeared in numerous anthologies. P.J. is also the co-founder of Red Cape Publishing.

Douglas Ford's fiction has appeared in *Dark Moon Digest*, *Diabolical Plots*, *Tales to Terrify*, along with several other small press publications. Past work has appeared in *The Best Hardcore Horror*, Volumes Three and Four, and a novella, *The Reattachment*, appeared in 2019 courtesy of Madness Heart Press. Other recent publications include a collection of short fiction from Madness Heart Press and a story set to appear in *The Half You See*.

Matt Henshaw (he/him) lives and works in Central IL with his wife and two cats. In addition to writing, Matt has also produced experimental and avant-garde music for over 25 years. You can learn more about Matt's creative output at http://getoutofjailfreemusic.blogspot.com.

Christine Morgan is a frazzled wreck who tries to escape her stress by writing really weird shit. This particular piece is not the first time she owes major apologies to P.G. Wodehouse. Her works include the deep-sea chompy Trench Mouth, the Splatterpunk Award winning Lakehouse Infernal, and the splatter western The Night Silver River Run Red.

Chandler Morrison is the author of *Human-Shaped Fiends, Along the Path of Torment, Dead Inside, Until the Sun, Hate to Feel,* and *Just to See Hell.* His short fiction has appeared in numerous anthologies and literary journals. He lives in Los Angeles.

Christian Saunders, who writes fiction as C.M. Saunders, is a freelance journalist and editor from south Wales. His work has appeared in almost 100 magazines, ezines and anthologies worldwide including Fortean Times, the Literary Hatchet, ParABnormal, Fantastic Horror, Haunted MTL, Feverish Fiction and Crimson Streets, and he has held staff positions at several leading UK magazines ranging from Staff Writer to Associate Editor. His books have been both traditionally and independently published, the latest release being Back from the Dead, a collection of Zombie-themed fiction.

Hadley Scherz-Schindler lives in St. Louis with her husband, collie, and occasionally some of her four children, who are in various stages of young adulthood. She has degrees in English and law. When she visits her mother and brother's family in Charlottesville, Virginia, she notices that the profusion of mountains and trees seems to hide something frightening.

Susan Snyder is a two-time Splatterpunk award nominated writer of horror fiction and poetry. Her debut poetry collection, *Broken Nails*, was nominated for a 2021 Elgin Award. She writes a weekly shark movie review blog called *Sharksploitation Sunday*. The book *Encyclopedia Sharksploitanica*, containing Susan's tongue-in-cheek reviews of 85 of the best and worst of shark cinema, was released in 2021 by Madness Heart Press.

Jay Wilburn is a Splatterpunk award nominated author with work in Best Horror of the Year volume 5. He livestreams short story writing at Twitch.tv/JayWilburn a few days a week. He has written over 500 stories and some of them are pretty fucking good.

Heinrich von Wolfcastle is an affiliate member of the Horror Writers Association and a member of the Great Lakes Association of Horror Writers. His work has appeared in multiple anthologies and magazines. Most recently, you can hear his story "Things in the Attic" presented on the Scare You to Sleep podcast. Though he lives the life of a recluse, he has been known to emerge from the shadows for Trick-or-Treaters on Halloween night.

MORE ANTHOLOGIES FROM MADNESS HEART PRESS

Trigger Warning: Body Horror
978-1386684350

Trigger Warning: Hallucinations
979-8598457054

Creeping Corruption
978-1790644766

Devour the Earth: A Kaiju Anthology
979-8566583624

Ghastly Gastronomy: A Horror Cookbook
9781087884905

American Cult
978-1076432445

www.ingramcontent.com/pod-product-compliance
Lightning Source LLC
Chambersburg PA
CBHW060749180626
46818CB00002B/510